D.S. LLITERAS

JERUSALEM'S RAIN

a novel

HAMPTON ROADS
PUBLISHING COMPANY, INC.

Cover design by Marjoram Productions
Cover photographic montage © 2003 Jonathan Friedman and
© 2003 Photo 24/Brand X Pictures/PictureQuest

Hampton Roads Publishing Company, Inc.
1125 Stoney Ridge Road
Charlottesville, VA 22902
434-296-2772
fax: 434-296-5096
e-mail: hrpc@hrpub.com
www.hrpub.com

If you are unable to order this book from your local
bookseller, you may order directly from the publisher.
Call 1-800-766-8009, toll-free.

Library of Congress Cataloging-in-Publication Data

Lliteras, D. S.
  Jerusalem's rain : a novel / D.S. Lliteras.
     p. cm.
ISBN 1-57174-340-5 (trade cloth : alk. paper)
1. Jesus Christ--Crucifixion--Fiction. 2. Peter, the Apostle,
Saint--Fiction. 3. Church history--Primitive and early church, ca.
30-600--Fiction. 4. Bible. N.T.--History of Biblical events--Fiction.
I. Title.
  PS3562.L68J47 2003
  813'.54--dc21

                                    2003006459

10 9 8 7 6 5 4 3 2 1
Printed on acid-free paper in the United States

DEDICATED

TO

DAWN BAILIFF

For suffering contains the secret of creation and its dimension of eternity; it can be pierced only from the inside.

—Elie Wiesel

I don't think of all the misery, but of all the beauty that still remains.

—Anne Frank

A hurtful act is the transference to others of the degradation that we bear in ourselves.

—Simone Weil

Tragedy is essentially an expression, not of despair, but of the triumph over despair and of confidence in the value of human life.

—Joseph Wood Krutch

There's something supremely sad about existence, something too ridiculous to face alone.

—DSL

CHAPTER 1

The Men

Jerusalem trembled under a premature darkness; it did not resemble twilight. Lightning cut deep streaks across the threatening sky and thunder boomed its frightening terror into the heart of a man whose back was pressed anxiously against a stucco wall on a deserted street.

"Lord God in heaven, please . . . please help me, Lord!"

Rain pelted his bearded face as he looked up into the dark sky with a wild desperation equal to the ferocity of the unrelenting circular wind.

"Oh, God, please help me! Give me the courage to stand with . . . with the women at the foot of his cross!"

A nearby window shutter broke loose from its side jamb and came crashing to the ground. He scurried several steps in the opposite direction, then breathlessly pressed himself against the wall again in response to the appearance of an approaching lamp held by someone struggling to protect its tiny flicker from the wind and the rain.

A familiar voice called to him from the direction of the lamp. "Peter. Peter? Is that you? Peter, it's me. Me! Philip."

Peter watched the figure move tentatively toward him.

"Peter. Answer me. Is that you?"

After tremendous effort, Peter managed to croak. "Yes."

Philip hastened to him. And as soon as the lamp's illumination brightened the distance between them, Peter was comforted to see relief in a friendly face.

Both men were struck dumb by the deficiency of each other's presence. They hovered closely over the fragment of light as if their lives depended on it and managed to create a tiny pocket of safety: a vacuous environment for the harassed flame to survive the tempestuous wind that persistently threatened to extinguish the lamp light, as well as scatter the disjointed thoughts from the two desperate beings who had nowhere else to go and nothing else to do but to protect this little flicker of light.

"I don't understand this kind of darkness. I don't . . . I don't understand this . . . this darkness!" Peter shivered to near convulsion, leaving Philip confused.

The fierce hysteria assaulting Peter was so intense that it seemed physical rather than mental in origin.

"Are you alright?"

"Don't be stupid! Look at me! I . . . I." Peter turned away from Philip and threw himself, face forward, against the wall; his arms were outstretched with his palms flat against the white-washed surface.

"Not so loud, Peter. There are legionnaires all over the city looking for trouble."

"Good. Good!"

"Shut up, shut up! They'll crucify the lot of us if we don't watch out."

Peter crumbled to his knees while he dragged his forehead and outstretched palms against the rough surface of the wall. "Maybe . . . maybe that will force me to have the courage to be at his side."

Philip knelt beside him in a quiet desperation. "Our Master is finished. There's nothing we can do for him, nothing—nothing but stand among the women in their sorrow."

"In their courage, you mean."

"Women's courage?" Philip sought the expedient comfort of contempt. "It's of a low quality, my friend."

"Low! Low?" Peter's back stiffened to the flippant remark. He turned his agonized countenance toward Philip, leaving the unexposed side of his face pressed against the wall, and spewed venom at him. "That so-called quality of low is something that's being shared between us and only us."

"Not me."

"Then me. Me!" Peter pushed himself away from

the wall and allowed himself to crumble to the ground. Then he rolled onto his left side and curled up into a loose ball. "It torments me!"

Philip's eyes widened with panic. "Shhh!"

"What I wouldn't give for this . . . this low, woman's, courage. Courage. Courage." Peter released a sigh that normally corresponded with tears, but his face was distorted with laughter.

Philip was frightened by this contradiction in behavior. "Control yourself, please, don't . . . don't be angry with yourself. I . . . I also ran away like a coward. See? Self-preservation. There's nothing wrong with that."

"Justify it any way you want."

There was a long and frightfully unsteady silence, which brought Philip closer to the edge of his own sense of guilt.

"The essence of free will is the mind." The flat tone in Peter's voice came from the dead.

Philip tentatively approached Peter and reached downward to touch him. But Philip pulled his sympathetic hand away when Peter began to wriggle like an injured snake. Philip backed away and waited for Peter to regain some form of composure.

"Believe in me," Peter said, as he uncoiled himself and stood up. His self-contempt grew as he approached Philip. "Believe in me," he muttered as he stepped into the full darkness in the middle of the street. He was suffocating with self-loathing. Then he grabbed his head with both hands as if he were trying to rip it off his body. "Believe in me!" he cried with his arms projecting perpendicularly from his head.

Philip saw somebody peek furtively through a partially opened window shutter. "Peter, please, your madness is bringing us closer to danger. You're rousing
people from their slumber."

"Who are you kidding? Nobody sleeps on a night
like this. Sleeping? No. There's too much fear in the
air."

Philip heard several pounding footsteps near the
intersection of the street. "Peter. Listen. There's no
telling who—"

"There he is, after him!" a voice called out at some
distance to the right side of the street corner.

"Come back here, you traitor!" another voice
added.

Peter stiffened with fear and paranoia. "I didn't
betray—"

"Shh, damn you!" Philip whispered vehemently.
"This is not about you!"

Peter crouched where he stood in the middle of the
street, while Philip hugged the nearby wall with his
smouldering lamp; the fragile flame had succumbed to
the elements. "Damn."

"What?"

"Nothing. Quiet." Philip set the extinguished lamp
on the ground.

They maintained a steady gaze in the direction of
the dark intersection until they were startled by an
intense series of lightning flashes, which lit up a wet,
frightened figure who had paused to the paralyzing
crack of thunder. The sky continued to flicker like a
harassed candle and illuminated the stranger's face: it

was Judas! Their Judas. He appeared confused, lost, anchored to that very spot with indecision. He started to go left, toward them, but stopped.

"What happened to the silver!" an angry voice demanded from a closer distance.

"Wait. That's Ganto's voice," Philip uttered as he felt the need to crouch along the wall to make a smaller figure of himself. He saw Peter drop into a prone position in the muddy street.

Philip turned his gaze back toward the street's intersection and caught another glimpse of Judas's desperation under a hostile night's sky that wouldn't allow him to vanish into its darkness.

Judas scurried to the right away from them just as several men reached the intersection. They turned in the same direction and pursued him without hesitation.

Peter crawled to the wall where Philip was crouched and sat up on his knees. The rain pelted both their faces and soaked their woolen tunics, making the fabric weigh heavily against their skins.

Both men studied the length of the street as if expecting something else to occur. They peered past the narrow street's archway, which was about thirty paces away into the refuse-strewn gutter. In it were bones of leftover meals, rotting trash, softened dung, and diluted urine. The wet walls accented the dirt stains caused by years of abuse and heavy traffic of beasts and men.

Peter spoke as if he were winded. "That was Judas."

"And Ganto in hot pursuit."

"What's happening there?"

"I don't know." Philip was bewildered. "But I think
. . . I think Judas dealt too closely with Ganto for my
liking."

"Judas dealt closely with too many hidden things,"
Peter snapped. "None of it was to my liking."

"But our Master seemed to encourage his activities—"

"And he was kissed for it!"

"I don't think it was betrayal, Peter."

"Bah! How do you know?"

"Because . . . because Judas told me."

"Get away. When?"

"Earlier. This evening. Long after the arrest."

"Then not long ago."

"What does it matter?"

"He kissed him!"

"To protect our Master, he told me. To protect him
from an assassin's dagger."

"Ridiculous."

"Judas stood his ground against me," Philip insisted.
"And . . . and I remember him standing his ground
between Jesus and those legionnaires before . . . before
I broke and ran."

"Bull."

"How would you know?" Philip challenged. "You
were already among the scattered!"

"Shut up. Shut up!" Peter shuddered. "I'm disgusting, alright? My constant fear is disgusting, see? I'm
acting like a common dog."

Philip tried to retract his condemnation. "You
weren't the only one. We all scattered."

"This . . . this wasn't supposed to . . . to happen,
no. No! Not to me."

Philip pressed the palm of his hand against Peter's back to calm him. "We're all frightened. We're all running."

"This wasn't supposed to happen, no. No. Not to me." Peter tried to regain his composure. "What happened to Bartholomew?"

Philip shrugged. "He was arrested."

"Are you sure?"

"With Barabbas. I saw it myself. They were led away by several legionnaires. Someone told me they were being taken to the Fortress of Antonia."

"Where?"

"To the Roman dungeons."

"Scattered." Peter massaged his forehead with his left hand. "We're all scattered like . . . like bits of rubbish strewn about at Gehenna. And the others?"

"I don't know. I've been much too frightened to stand in one place long enough to find out. Bartholomew and Barabbas were only a frightened glimpse from the left side of my eyes."

"Then—"

"A definite and clear glimpse, I assure you, Peter."

"Damn. This . . . this crucifixion—"

"Has made cowards of us all, I tell you."

"No. Not made, has . . . has uncovered. Yes. Uncovered the cowardice in us all, all."

"You're being much too hard on us and—"

"Uncovered! We've been cowards all along, I say!"

"But our Master chose—"

"Hypocrites and idiots." Peter chuckled uncontrollably. "Don't try to soften my self-contempt. I won't have it!"

8

"We all run away from our past," Philip stated firmly.

Peter was close to shedding tears again. "I couldn't stay awake. On his last hour of prayer, I . . . we . . . I couldn't stay awake!"

"Don't be so tough on yourself," Philip pleaded.

"The hour for being tough has passed."

Philip shied away from his powerful companion. "I won't accept your condemnation or your perceptions."

"It's the only real truth I've come to understand since we've met Jesus."

"Oh, you, of so little faith."

"Oh, you, who shares with me the same shadows to hide and tremble in—get away from me." Peter grabbed Philip by the front of his tunic, spun him around once, and watched him tumble to the ground with a splash when he released him.

Philip stood up, dripping with mud and diluted urine. He was furious and ready to fight. "At least I did not verbally deny my association with our Master to anyone who challenged me."

"Thrice! Only three times!"

"And not a breath's difference from thirty-three hundred times." The tone in Philip's voice was cruel and vicious.

"Damn your eyes!" Peter struck Philip on the jaw with his right fist. "Yes, I denied him." Then he struck him with a left. "I denied him like a dog, you bastard." Then Peter proceeded to beat him without mercy.

Philip parried the next set of blows but was taken off guard by Peter's kick in the gut. He involuntarily hunched forward and pressed his forearms against his abdomen as he purposely leaned to the right and hit the ground on a roll in order to get out of harm's way. But Peter's violent temper had become so aggressive that there was no time for Philip to fully recover his breath. Philip stood up on his left knee, which was balanced by the firm plant of his right foot, and prepared a counterattack by waiting for Peter to initiate another assault. And when Peter's blurred figure started his menacing approach, Philip waited for the precise moment to lunge toward him like a ram. He struck Peter in the gut with his right shoulder.

Both men exhaled with great pain upon collision. They collapsed where they stood, still joined at their points of impact, gasping for air.

Peter recovered first. He issued a double-fisted blow against the side of Philip's head, then rolled away from him. When he rose unsteadily to his feet, he was surprised to see Philip standing.

"I'm going to kill you, Philip."

"Bark, bark, you mangy dog."

"I'll crush you like the worm you've always been!"

The sanity that these two men had once shared no longer existed. Instead of his usual appeasement, Philip taunted Peter into greater fury; instead of being the rock of self-control, Peter was the lava of mad fury and hurt pride.

Peter approached Philip with deliberate hard-hearted meanness; his intent to destroy was clear.

Philip was startled by the ferocity in Peter's eyes. "My God. Is that me? Have we become?—"

Peter struck Philip with a deaf brutality worthy of a professional legionnaire.

Philip withstood the heavy blow, which surprised Peter into a standstill. Both men heaved breathlessly like a couple of exhausted bulls as they studied each other.

They came from similar stock. Both men were natives of Bethsaida of Galilee. But that's where their likenesses parted.

Philip was a smart man who went by a Greek name. He was usually coolheaded and rational and extremely practical toward acquiring the material needs that were necessary for his relative comfort, which eased some of the weariness that accompanied a life on the road with a small band of men and women who followed the charismatic Jesus—their Master. His proclivity toward trade and acquisition brought him closer to Judas, who held the communal purse. He'd grown used to dealing with Judas's difficult temperament and considered his ability to smooth out Judas's erratic behavior as one of the talents he was chosen for by his Master. But Philip had grown weary of Judas's mercurial personality and paranoia, which eventually manifested in an argumentative relationship. Philip was hesitant, Judas was haphazard; Philip was slow toward spiritual realizations, Judas was quick to believe and disbelieve; simply, Philip knew too much arithmetic to be easily convinced by magic.

Philip's head and facial hair was shorter but thicker than Peter's. His face was pinched, forehead narrow, and features drawn close together, which gave him a worried introspective appearance. He was quite approachable, despite his scholarly demeanor and his massive barrel-chested size that was more bulk than muscle; this made his physical stature almost equal to his present opponent.

Peter was all brawn, natural by birth and tempered by years as a fisherman. The addition of his hothead-edness made him both a gentle and dangerous man who always approached everything with a big begin-ning. He was a man with great spiritual ambition, a man who could not rest until the end of a task was reached, a man who could not walk away from another man's challenge, which is why he was snorting and spit-ting in Philip's direction.

Both men were strong-willed and uncompromising in their world view and, therefore, fragile with pride. They were standing before each other fully committed to destroy themselves.

A slash of lightning slit the black sky so deeply that it must have cut its underside as if it were a bag of water.

Peter was caught off guard by the strength of Philip's backhanded insult across his right cheek, which made him stagger several steps backward. The blow dazed him for several seconds, leaving him defenseless to Philip's openhanded smack followed by a left jab and a right uppercut to his jaw. Peter was too strong to be brought down with only one strong blow in four. But his mind was clouded and he was left bleeding from the nose and at the corner of his mouth. Peter ran the back of his left arm and hand against his face and felt the wetness of his blood to assess his injuries. This prompted him to shake off his bewilderment and launch a serious attack.

The brutish impact of their bodies immobilized their wills and forced them to recognize the pain. Both men dropped to their knees gasping for air; their eyes were wide with panic. Peter tried to maneuver his arm around his opponent's neck, but Philip squirmed away from the intended hold and countered with an ineffective body slam. Peter grabbed him by the waist and, with a slight lift, began squeezing him with a crushing hug. Philip responded to Peter's strength with a determined struggle powerful enough to bring both men to the ground in a desperate series of left and right rolls in the muddy street. To Philip's surprise, he was on top when they relaxed their embrace and ceased rolling— they were covered with the stench of the street.

Peter smashed Philip in the face with his forehead, then pulled Philip's limp figure off to one side. He watched Philip roll several times on the ground until he splashed face down in the mud.

With tremendous difficulty, Peter sat up expecting Philip to retaliate. But Philip remained face down, floating on the surface of the flooded street composed of rain and dust and excrement.

Peter wiped the rain from his face. "Get up, damn it! Get up!" He floundered to his hands and knees, alarmed by Philip's inertness. "I'm not finished with you!" He anxiously crawled toward the body. "I said get up!"

Philip raised his head and upper body from the water, gasping and coughing and splashing desperately for air. But as soon as he saw Peter, he began to curse and spit madly at him. Infected by the contagious rage,

Peter grabbed Philip by his tunic's midriff and pulled him sideways along the slick street. Philip glided on his knees long enough to recover his equilibrium, then lifted his left leg and planted his heel so he could rise to his feet. They were both startled by the caustic expression in each other's face made worse by a streak of lightning across the threatening sky.

Philip struck Peter with his fist, turned away, and began to run toward the street's intersection. The varying depths in the puddles made running difficult; he stumbled several times. Then he panicked with indecision after he reached the crossroad and heard Peter's footsteps splashing in pursuit. Philip veered right and ran close to the wall for upright support with his nearest hand. He stumbled on a pile of trash and fell headlong into the gutter. He had just enough time to recover and stand up to face Peter's unrelenting attack.

The blow to Philip's ear forced him to turn full circle, which disoriented him long enough to receive a straight punch to the face; his nose spurted blood. Philip pressed the heel of his left hand near the cleft of his nose while he swung his open right hand around and clawed Peter's face.

Peter yelped as Philip dug his fingers into one of his eyes, as well as up one nostril. The assault was so disabling that Peter frantically bit Philip's pinkie to the bone. They released each other simultaneously and backed away nursing their wounds: Peter, his eye; Philip, his finger.

The sound of rain grew louder with the rise of standing water; its flow, cascading from rooftops and running down second-story stairways, accentuated the barren feeling of the deserted streets. Guarded eyes could be felt piercing through the darkness from behind cracked shutters and jarred doorways. Ordinarily, local street disturbances by outsiders were confronted immediately by the inhabitants. But Jerusalem's city dwellers were saturated this evening with strange weather and nervous behavior along with increased rebels, bandits, and Roman military presence. The city's labyrinth of empty streets possessed the power to make all vagabonds feel the dread of infinite hopelessness. Even the open porticoes and verandas could not provide adequate shelter against the constant, changing wind and rain.

The ground shuddered as the sky rumbled with a reverberating thunder that grew closer during its progress across the land. Under a portico, several gourds that were hanging from a rafter in a cluster rattled softly against each other while a small clay pot vibrated along the top of a nearby bench.

Peter peered at these articles from a stooped position; his protective fist, supported by the palm of his other hand, was pressed against his injured eye. The objects clattered and vibrated and taunted him with their inanimate indifference—he began to sob. He dragged his fist down to his cheek, then past the jaw, and held it against his upper chest with his other hand as he straightened his back and arched his neck. He did not sound like a man when he hollered and he did not sound like any known beast.

Philip was startled by the intensity of Peter's agony.

He brought his left hand, which still had three of its lower fingers wrapped around his wounded right pinkie, to his trembling mouth in a gesture of self-control. He wanted to scream, but Peter's verbal malediction kept him in a mild, silent shock.

"Damn you, Lord! Save me! Save me from this . . . this, my denial. Take it back, please! I will lay down my life for your sake!" Peter slapped himself. "I don't know this man. I don't know this man. I don't know this man!" He slapped himself harder after each denial. Then he looked at Philip and realized that his companion had observed him at his worst. He wept bitterly.

From a rooftop, someone threw a well-aimed rock that hit Peter on the temple and knocked him to his knees.

"Get away from here, you wretch!" a voice called out. "Take your troubles to another part of the city!"

Peter stood up and craned his neck in several directions in an effort to locate the voice. "Come out, come out! I'll kill you, you scum!" But he saw Philip instead.

Philip understood the danger he was facing. He wanted to square off with Peter and slug it out with him to put an end to this madness. But Peter was unhinged by his series of denials, and a simple fight was not going to exhaust his self-contempt.

Philip had been a witness to only one denial—a simple incident caused by an accusing old woman. But Peter had caught sight of Philip's surprise and thought it must have been in judgment of him. Judgment.

"I did not judge you!" Philip shouted.

"I saw what I saw."

"It was my own silence. My own guilt! Not yours that you saw. I don't make a good witness."

"Your continued existence makes you so." Peter made a move toward Philip.

"No. No!" Philip lost his defiant posture and ran like a guilty man.

Peter doggedly pursued him down several long streets, even though he knew Philip was too fast for him.

Philip made a right turn into a narrow back street and ran at top speed to increase his distance from Peter. But to his surprise, the street came to a dead end. He was trapped and on the verge of panic. He stopped and turned in several directions to study his surroundings.

A carpenter's shed with an attached veranda stood to his right; it was part of the dwelling behind him. To his left, there was a high stucco wall, two floors in height and windowless.

Philip spun completely around in an act of mad desperation. Tears ran down his cheeks. Confusion crippled his reason. Terror threw him into isolation. Anger reduced him to essentials. His finger throbbed.

He approached the tidy carpenter's shed in search for what? A weapon? Was this the universal object of reduction? The distilled response to terror? The mandatory defense against terror? The only answer to confusion? His tears continued to flow without emotion as he searched the darkness under the carpenter's veranda.

Philip's back stiffened when his foot brushed against the wooden object. He stooped over and

17

grabbed it with both hands, breathlessly scurried toward the darkest wall, and pressed his back against it for support. The object was a short piece of lumber no thicker than the grip of a hand. He brought the object close to his chest and hugged the impotent staff. He hated the smell of fear. He hated himself.

By tilting the staff crosswise, he transformed it into a weapon. Philip pushed himself away from the wall and stepped out from under the carpenter's veranda to meet Peter's onslaught. "Don't come any closer!"

Peter had begun a cautious search of the area when he heard Philip's challenge. He hesitated when he saw the outline of Philip's figure appear from a darker part of the night. Warily, he circled to Philip's left. "Where did you get that?" His labored breathing was accentuated by wheezing.

"I'll use this against you, I swear."

Peter laughed. "You'd better!"

Philip swung the length of wood at Peter to demonstrate its potential.

"You'll have to do better than that," Peter taunted. "You swing a club like a woman."

Peter backed away and shuffled along a nearby wall to conduct a search. Philip quietly stood by, licked his dry lips, and considered fleeing again. In fact, he was about to throw down his weapon and run when he heard Peter gasp with delight.

"We're equal." Peter brandished a piece of lumber with zeal. He cradled it in the palms of both hands and quickly transformed the length of wood into a weapon by pointing it at Philip like a pilum.

Philip stepped toward him in defense. "You could be mistaken for a legionnaire."

The insult ignited Peter. He lunged at Philip with his pilum and missed Philip's side by one finger's width.

After a belated parry, Philip lowered his pilum to hip level. "I can play legionnaire as well."

They circled each other like two gladiators waiting for an opening move, looking for a crippling blow. Both men stalked with a primal skill inherited before birth; their basic instincts were stripped to nakedness. Into raw emotions. Hard eyes. Torn reason. Chiseled faces—all—internals born from the external events of their present: the betrayals, the denials, the crucifixion of their Master—all—had carved new features into these men.

Peter aimed his first thrust at Philip's face and almost struck him in the eye. Philip managed to avoid the injury by pulling back so quickly that he lost his balance and slipped onto the muddy street. The fall was so dramatic and unexpected that he helplessly dropped his stick upon impact. By the time he sat up, Peter was standing over him preparing to club him with the length of wood. Philip lifted his left arm above his head in self-defense and waited for the blow. But another rock was hurled from a rooftop and struck Peter in the back of the head.

Peter's face went blank. He released the club, dropped to his knees, and fell face down into the muddy street.

Philip scrambled to his feet and circled past Peter's

inert body toward the entrance of the street. He wanted to get away from this horror—to simply get away! But he couldn't. He couldn't let Peter drown. He took a deep breath and ran his fingers through his wet hair. The rain, the rain—this relentless rain! He turned and reluctantly sloshed toward Peter.

Alarmed by the body's absolute stillness, Philip knelt beside him, grabbed Peter's shoulder, and rolled him to his side. To Philip's horror, Peter reached for Philip's throat with a powerful hand and began strangling him.

Philip punched him in the gut with all his might and managed to pull away from Peter when his hand went slack. He stood up, unsure of his balance, and began to run toward the entrance of the street.

"Come back here and fight me," Peter hollered. "Come back!"

Philip wouldn't look back for fear of losing his balance. He half-stumbled and half-ran while half-blinded by the rain, the darkness, the strain. And he was half-shocked when he collided with two men.

"Make way. Get out of my way!" Philip demanded.

"Is that you, Philip?"

The sound of his name from a friendly voice overwhelmed him to the point of tears. "Andrew?"

"Yes."

"Andrew?"

"It's me and Thaddaeus."

Philip slumped against Andrew, who responded with a supportive embrace.

"Steady, my friend."

Philip wept fitfully. "Your brother, he's . . .

20

he's gone mad . . . mad with grief and . . . and self-contempt."

"You mean, Peter?" Thaddaeus interjected. "Where?"

"Back . . . back there," Philip lamented.

Thaddaeus started down the street toward the dead end.

"Wait! Thaddaeus!" Philip grabbed him by his tunic. "He's mad, I tell you!"

"I've never been afraid of his temper."

"No! This is . . . it's not temperament."

"I know, I know. It's still Peter."

"No!" Philip was hysterical.

"Easy, my friend," Andrew said, as he adjusted his embrace to console Philip.

Philip disentangled himself from Andrew and pushed him away. "You don't understand."

"What?"

"Your brother." Philip pointed into the dark void of the dead-end street. "Your brother! In there. His . . . his madness is . . . is contagious. And horrible. Look at me. Believe me. Look at me!"

"I don't see any leprosy," Thaddaeus retorted.

Andrew's laughter, in response to Thaddaeus's halfhearted jest, was strained.

"You idiots! You don't understand!"

Andrew attempted another embrace, but Philip squirmed away from him. "Control yourself, Philip. Herod's police—"

"And Roman legionnaires—" said Thaddaeus.

"Yes! Are everywhere tonight. It's not safe."

Philip leaned against a wall and cackled hysterically. "He's dead. He's dead! What will we do now? What—" Philip's lips trembled. "Did . . . did either of you stay?" He peered at Andrew. "Did . . . did you accompany, no, did . . . did you stand at the foot of his cross?"

Andrew lowered his head in shame. "I fled. I . . . I fled for my life."

"Thaddaeus?"

Unable to gaze into Philip's inquiring eyes, Thaddaeus shifted his weight from one leg to the other and exhaled uneasily. "I . . . I simply fled."

"Lord. Our Jesus." Philip shook his head. "You mean, he died alone?"

"And sadly, I think," Thaddaeus confessed.

"And without us," Andrew added with embarrassment.

"There had to be somebody," Philip said plaintively.

"Yes. I'm sure."

"But not us. Not us."

The intimacy of their shame drew them physically closer to each other. The raw silence between them and the easing of the thunderstorm intensified their emotional nakedness.

Their mud-stained tunics were in tatters and clung heavily to their skins. They reeked of ammonia caused by an excess of nervous perspiration. Their sandals, toes, and ankles were laden with mud and fecal matter, which adhered to their feet like clay. As they held their breaths, they silently consoled each other at eye level.

Andrew's upper mantle was wrapped around his

neck and tied thickly in place with a hasty knot, which drooped heavily against his chest. His hair was pulled back and tied together with a piece of leather, and his heavy beard and mustache were cut short and square to accentuate his angular features. The overall effect was a handsome chiseled face that appeared fiercer than the man himself.

In direct physical contrast, Thaddaeus was a mess. His scraggly, unkempt beard did not fully conceal his facial pockmarks and his chronic rash. His features were very large: thick lips, humped nose, and huge round eyes set too far apart and crowned with bushy eyebrows. His long hair fell to shoulder length in a tangle of curls in back and, in front, it covered his short forehead with an unruly bang, which behaved like an inverted cowlick.

Their moment together was brief, but the shared guilt was eternal. The exposed impotence left them paralyzed and vulnerable and stunned by Peter's unexpected and explosive attack. The lot of them tumbled heavily to the ground in a tangled heap.

"He's mad, I told you!" Philip crawled away from his floundering brethren, dazed and too exhausted to run.

"Peter! It's me. Your brother! Andrew." He pushed and squirmed underneath Thaddaeus and Peter's weight. "Get off me, you idiot. Wait! What are you doing? Philip, look out! Peter's taken my knife!"

Thaddaeus grabbed Peter by one of his legs. "For heaven's sake, control yourself!" Peter kicked him in the lower back with his other foot. "Agh, damn you!"

He released Peter's leg. "Watch it, Philip! He's gotten free of us!"

Philip was terrified by Peter's unbridled madness. "For God's sake, help me!" He remained squat, on flat feet, still too exhausted to run from this armed maniac. He plunged his right hand into the flooded street and scooped up a clump of mud as Peter sloshed toward him brandishing the knife. One shot at his target was all he was going to get. So, he waited and waited and waited until he was certain: he stood up and flung the mud into Peter's face.

Peter hollered in a blind rage as he stumbled to his left in a small circle. He slashed the darkness with his knife while he wiped the mud from his eyes with his free hand. "Nothing will save you!"

"Nothing will save us!" Philip countered.

In despair, Peter rented the front of his tunic and exposed his hairy chest to the torrential rain. "No amount of water can cleanse me! No! Not present! Not present! I wasn't present at his sacrifice!"

Andrew and Thaddaeus rushed Peter from behind and almost succeeded in knocking the weapon out of his hand.

"Come to your senses," Andrew cried.

"Listen to your own blood, even if you don't choose to count me as your brother," Thaddaeus pleaded.

Peter wasn't listening. He struggled against them with the unchecked power of madness supplying him with the strength of several men.

Philip was through running. "Our Rabbi's death is not about you, Peter. It's not always about you!"

Peter dragged both men with him as he approached Philip.

"Come on! Show me more of your cowardice." Philip recklessly stepped toward Peter. "Show us—"

Peter wildly thrust the knife at Philip and managed to stab him in the side, as he stumbled and fell from the persistent weight of the other two men.

Philip's facial expression flattened with shock before he cried with disbelief. "I've been stabbed. God! I've been cut!"

The knife had gone through the fleshiest portion of his midriff in front, well into the muscle, and had come out through the back. Peter had been forced to release the handle amid his struggle with the other two disciples, leaving the knife fully skewered into Philip's side.

Blood flowed gently from his wound on both sides. Pain and shock launched Philip into a macabre dance, which expressed panic and disorientation and several interpretations of hysteria.

Andrew and Thaddaeus continued their struggle against Peter. They wrestled him to the ground and tentatively managed to restrain him; they tried to reason with him.

A flurry of invectives was Peter's response along with a renewed struggle.

Exasperated, Andrew struck his brother several times in the jaw and the stomach and the side of his face until the continuous violence took physical effect.

Peter went limp, but remained conscious. "God, my God, why have you forsaken me!"

"Shut up, you big selfish idiot!" Thaddaeus had had

enough. He released Peter and stood up. "Why have you forsaken us? And now, most of all, Philip." He went to Philip's writhing figure and guided him to a wall for some pretense of protection against Peter and the weather.

Philip touched the handle of the knife. "Take it out. It hurts. Take it out."

Thaddaeus made him sit down. "Lean against the wall. That's it. Good." He peered at Andrew. "The knife has got to come out. I need your help."

Andrew released Peter. "You start your madness again and I swear, I swear I'll show you no mercy. I swear by our Master's name, Jesus, that I'll . . . I'll—" He stood up, looked down at Peter with disgust, then spat on the ground.

"Forget him already! Come help me with Philip."

Andrew left Peter lying face up in the mud. "What can I do to help?"

"Hold him against the wall."

"I . . . I don't need to be held. I can take care of my own pain."

"Easy, Philip. It's not only about pain." Thaddaeus inspected the knife. "I don't want you flinching too much when I pull this thing out of you. I'm trying to avoid further damage." He placed the flat of his left hand against Philip's abdomen, with his thumb and forefinger pressed around the wound, as he grabbed hold of the knife handle with his right. He glanced at Thaddaeus. "Hold him."

Thaddaeus genuflected on the other side of Philip and arranged himself so that his right leg was crossed over Philip's ankles, his left knee was resting against

Philip's right side, and his hands were pressing Philip's shoulders against the wall.

Andrew adjusted himself accordingly, then tried to smile at Philip. "Like I said, it's not only about pain. But this is going to hurt." He looked at Thaddaeus. "Ready?"

"I hope so."

Andrew swiftly pulled out the knife without further warning.

The shock in Philip's face preceded his short yelp. He remained conscious.

Andrew studied his knife. "I never thought this would ever be used for anything but scraping scales and filleting fish." He cast the implement into the darkness. When he heard it splash, he shuddered. "I loathe this day."

"We need to do something about this bleeding," Thaddaeus cautioned.

"Right." Andrew untied his upper mantle from around his neck. "Where's yours?"

"Lost it somewhere."

"And, apparently, so has Philip. Well, then . . . this will have to do."

"You . . . you can have mine," Peter uttered in a husky voice. He towered above them like a retarded giant.

"My, my, look who's back among the sane."

"Careful, Thaddaeus. That could be a ghost of himself."

"A ghost is all that's left of me," Peter confessed.

"I don't care, my brother. I don't have time to listen."

Peter knelt among them with his offering. "Take my mantle, please."

"Take it," Philip insisted. "Take the damn thing."

"Alright, alright. But squeeze the water out first," Andrew instructed. "Then fold it into a dressing. Thaddaeus."

"What?"

"Shift Philip toward you and support him from behind. We've got to raise his tunic to his chest."

Philip did not resist the maneuver, even though it was painful. Andrew and Thaddaeus worked in concert to stop the bleeding while Peter looked on in silence.

Andrew took the dressing from Peter, which was long enough to press the front edge against the entry wound and press the back edge against the exit wound with its thickness. Thaddaeus, who had Philip cradled between his arms and legs with Philip's back resting against his supportive chest, was able to hold the dressing in place while Andrew used his own mantle as a bandage. After Andrew wrapped the bandage around Philip's waist, he tied the knot against the uninjured side.

"There. That's the best I can do." Andrew pulled Philip's tunic down to his thighs and helped Thaddaeus reposition him back against the wall.

Thaddaeus sat next to Philip for added support. "What do we do now?"

"He could use your wife's nursing."

"I'm alright. I'll be fine."

"Nobody's asking you," Andrew scolded.

"Mara can nurse him," Peter said cautiously.

Andrew shot a hard glance at his brother. "You've done enough for one night."

"Easy, my friend," Thaddaeus warned. "We don't need any more fighting."

"They can all nurse me," Philip said.

Thaddaeus glanced at Peter. "I hope our women and children have managed to find their way back to Aaron's dwelling. Wasn't his home near the place we suppered last with our Master?"

"Yes."

"And the others," Andrew wondered. "I hope they're safely dispersed elsewhere for the night."

"Yes, yes, I'm sure they're fine." Philip was becoming impatient. "Let's go somewhere dry and safe. A woman's care will be welcomed."

"Right." Andrew regained command of the situation. "You're right. Which way is it?"

"That way," Peter said.

Andrew wiped some mud from Philip's face. "Can you stand?"

"I think so."

"But can he walk?" Thaddaeus added.

"We'll see soon enough. Help me up." Philip grunted and winced. "Easy. There." He was shaky but on his feet, with Andrew and Thaddaeus on either side and Peter standing before him. "Well. What have you got to say for yourself?" Peter was saddened with remorse. "Good. Say nothing more. We're ridiculous, and only silence will prevent it from getting worse." He took several small steps with their assistance before letting go of Andrew. "I'm fine." But he would have fallen without Thaddaeus's support. "Which way?"

"This way," Peter said sheepishly, as he led the way.

The rain had slowed to a drizzle. Thunder rumbled in the distance. The darkness flickered from the lightning of another region. A few stars escaped from behind the sky's thickness.

Grateful for the respite, they carefully plodded toward their destination.

Andrew was the first of them to hear the approach of the legionnaires. "Wait. Against the wall. Quick!"

The four of them scrambled to the nearest wall and tried to hide beside its darkness. They made too much noise.

"Who goes there?" one of the legionnaires summoned.

"Damn, we've been heard," Peter whispered.

They held their breaths and continued to press themselves into the darkness as the legionnaires entered the far end of the same street in plain view. There were eight soldiers in a loose, double-column formation lumbering in their direction.

"The one in front and on the left must be their leader," Peter whispered.

"How come?"

"Because see?—there again, he pointed in our direction—here they come."

"Damn legionnaires."

"Auxiliary troops, I think."

"No, no, garrison guards! Can't you tell by their helmets?"

30

"No matter." Thaddaeus spat on the ground. "They're all the same to me."

Andrew nudged Philip's arm. "Are you alright?"

"I'm fine, really."

"I said, who goes there!"

"Quick. Somebody think of something," Andrew whispered.

"Be drunk."

"What?"

"Act drunk!" Thaddaeus cupped his hands over his mouth.

"Shhh!"

They heard a sword being removed from its scabbard. "I won't call you out again!"

Andrew nervously slapped Thaddaeus on the shoulder. "Sing something, big mouth!"

"Me?! Sing what?"

"Anything!"

Philip precipitously bellowed the beginning words to a song and encouraged the others to join him.

Peter laughed raucously and stumbled capriciously into the middle of the street. "Behold! An off-tune musical refrain is no better than a cup of cheap wine!"

"Yeow!" Thaddaeus also pretended to be drunk and encouraged Andrew to follow along. Together, they joined Peter in the middle of the street, with Philip held between them as if he were too drunk to stand alone.

The legionnaires approached them with extreme caution. "Halt, right there," said the one in charge. He directed his men into a loose defense formation. "Stand as you are, I say!"

The disciples feigned surprise to see the legionnaires.

"What . . . what have we here?" Thaddaeus openly said in jest. "Romans? Or Syrians?"

The soldier in charge stepped toward them brandishing his double-edged sword. "Watch your tongue or you'll soon find out!"

Thaddaeus unsteadily bowed in obeisance realizing he may have stepped across the line of humor into insult. "Sorry. So, so sorry."

The legionnaires glared at Thaddaeus for a long, chilling moment. "What are you, the lot of you, doing out on a night like this?"

Unable to provide a verbal response, the four of them swayed with faked intoxication and laughed with great exaggeration. Thaddaeus hastily released Philip and took several unsure steps before he turned away from both groups of men.

"What are you doing?" the soldier demanded, his sword slightly raised.

"I'm taking a piss!" Thaddaeus increased the slur in his speech. "Anything . . . anything wrong . . . wrong with that?"

Some of the other legionnaires began to laugh. One of them addressed their section leader. "They're just out on a drunk, sergeant. Look at them. They're smashed."

"Which is about the only sensible thing to do on a night like this," another soldier added.

"Who can blame them? I mean, who among us wouldn't appreciate a bowl of posca right now?"

Several members of the formation enthusiastically agreed.

Their sergeant softened. "I suppose you're right." He lowered his sword. "In fact, they're the first sensible Jews I've met all night."

Thaddaeus executed a superb pratfall as soon as he was done urinating. "Crap! Slipped on my own piss!"

The legionnaires and the disciples laughed heartily at Thaddaeus's drunken antics.

"That one would have made an excellent legionnaire!" one of the soldiers in formation shouted.

"Alright, alright," the sergeant intervened, demanding order among the ranks and silence from the disciples. He resheathed his sword, then directed his advice to the biggest of them, Peter.

"You and your cohorts seem steady to me. But this is an ominous night and the guards are out in force. I suggest you go—"

"To an all night tavern!"

"Trakas!" The sergeant turned to the young legionnaire. "I said shut up!" The others in the formation stifled their laughter. The sergeant addressed all the disciples. "Go home—wherever that is." He took a deep breath for effect. "Out of the kindness of my heart, I'm going to ignore you sensible sots." In response to his hand gesture, the soldiers fell back into their double column. He joined them at the head of the formation and addressed the four swaying men one last time. "I don't want to see any of you again tonight. The lot of you will smell the inside of a dungeon if I do." With a nod, he dismissed them from his attention and issued the next command to his men with another hand gesture. The loose formation lumbered past the four bewildered men in the same way they had approached them.

The astonished disciples stood as motionless as statues. They no longer swayed or breathed. They no longer had animated expressions.

Andrew waited until the legionnaires were far enough not to hear them. "Thaddaeus, that performance was almost too much."

Philip actually giggled.

"Maybe." Thaddaeus grinned. "But we got away with it."

"Praise God." Peter snickered.

"Praise Thaddaeus's comic abilities," Philip amended. His giggling was contagious and it broadened into laughter among them.

"My God. What are we doing?" Peter gasped. "Should we be laughing so soon after our Lord's execution?"

"Ease up, already," Philip said. "Rabbi Jesus would have been the first to have laughed with us here."

"That's right." Thaddaeus readjusted his loincloth. "Enough of your ponderous mind, Peter. Enough. But . . . but what do we do now?"

"I say let's get away from here before those legionnaires return," Andrew said.

"Or maybe," Philip proposed, while slowly developing an idea, "maybe it's time we go to Golgotha."

"Golgotha!" Thaddaeus's eyes grew wide. "That's sheer madness."

"Has it been anything else this night?"

"But are . . . are you up to it, Philip?"

"Look at me, Andrew. I'm already standing on my own. See? And the bleeding has stopped."

"You're serious." Thaddaeus pressed the palm of his left hand against his forehead to express his dismay. "The two of you are really serious."

"And they're right," Peter added. "There's nothing else for us to lose."

"Right," Thaddaeus said, while nodding his head facetiously. "Nothing to lose but our lives."

"We're nothing to anybody anymore." Philip pointed in the direction of the departed legionnaires. "There's the proof. We just encountered Rome and, look, we're still free."

Andrew's merriment dissolved. "As long as we keep silent and hide like rats, you mean."

"Only . . . only for tonight," Peter said hopefully.

"Who are you kidding?" said Andrew, with disdain. "For as long as it takes to avoid crucifixion, you mean."

The group slumped into depression.

"I haven't uttered a single prayer since our—" Peter was too distressed to go on.

Philip pressed his left hand against his side to support his wound before taking a step; he separated himself from the others in order to face them. "I'm as guilty as the rest of you. And I'll admit, I'm still afraid for my life. But this inner torment, I . . . I've got to ease some of this torment." He shook his head and snorted with self-contempt. "What selfishness. See? Even this confession concerns only me: my pain, my death, my shame. Not his. Not—" He licked his lips. "I hate myself as much as you do yourselves. As much as—" he glanced at Peter, unable to go on.

They stood in the middle of an empty Jerusalem street for an undetermined period of time. The rain had ceased. The sky was calmer. The silence was fuller.

Thaddaeus approached Philip and offered him a supportive arm. "Can I join you in this insanity?"

"Of course."

"Then take hold of my arm and lean against me."

Andrew stirred from his bowed attitude. "I'll lead the way." He gazed at Peter. "Are you coming with us?"

Peter yielded to a forlorn stretch, which eased some of his physical stress. "It would be suicide for me not to go there with you. Besides, I know the way." Peter joined Andrew and waited to see if Philip could really travel. Philip's expression did not change when their eyes met long enough for Peter to transmit a silent apology.

Thaddaeus provided Philip with steady and effective support, and Peter provided Andrew with reliable directions. They proceeded with caution, but with resolve, toward the place of the skull: a wretched place of shattered dreams and lost causes, a place of pain and suffering, and a place, most of all, of annihilation and death.

They saw a dim light burning from a lantern as they approached the needle's eye.

Damascus Gate was a large stone edifice with a tower on either side of an architectural arch designed into a high wall. The arch encased a square entrance to a wide, fifteen cubits-long corridor that led to a massive wooden gate at the other end. Built into that closed main gate was the needle's eye, a small wooden door that allowed limited access into and out of the city at night.

The flame of the oil lamp flickered more noticeably from within the protection of its enclosed hanging lantern the closer they got to the mouth of the gate's corridor. A figure stirred under the circle of its light upon hearing their approaching footsteps.

"Don't frighten the gatekeeper," Peter cautioned. "They're a touchy lot."

"Who goes there?" the gatekeeper anxiously hailed.

"We're lost pilgrims." Peter led the other three into the dimly lit passageway. "Don't be alarmed."

The corridor was dry and empty except for a sleeping beggar. Its relative comfort reminded the disciples of their cold, miserable condition and emphasized their debased appearance. The torn and ragged band behaved as skittishly as a pack of mistreated dogs. None of this escaped the gatekeeper's attention.

"You must be broke as well to be seeking refuge outside the city walls on such a dreary night."

"Ahh, you've seen through us already, sir," Peter said with forced amiability.

Andrew hurried alongside Peter and offered the gatekeeper the reassurance of his genuine smile. "Peace be with you." The gatekeeper acknowledged him with a friendly but suspicious nod. "You . . . you wouldn't have a spare lamp or, perhaps, a humble torch that we can borrow?"

"Even a torch, you say? To borrow, you ask?" The gatekeeper chortled nervously. "No. No, no. I'm sorry. There are far too many transients who seek a loan or even a purchase of a torch for me to accommodate them." He pointed to his own hanging lamp. "Oil. Strictly oil caged in my lantern."

"I see," Andrew said. "I'm surprised there isn't more than one beggar taking refuge within these walls."

"It's an ominous night, pilgrim. Everybody seems to have scurried into private holes. They're hiding from unsympathetic police and legionnaires who seem to be arresting everyone in sight. It's that and, well, this very strange weather is frightening, don't you think? Where has it come from?" The gatekeeper sidled closer to Andrew and Peter for dramatic effect. "I've heard rumors." He lowered his voice. "There are those who believe that one of those crucified at Golgotha is the cause of this bleakness and tumult. Some say he was a magician. Others think, a sorcerer. That is, if any of his rumored powers are really true."

"The one you speak about is neither a magician or a sorcerer, my friend," Philip said. "The one you speak of is Jesus of Nazareth."

"Woe, Nazareth." The gatekeeper peered around Peter to catch sight of Philip. "They say nothing good ever comes out of Nazareth."

"Who's they?"

"Well, you know. *They*."

"Ah," said Philip, pretending to understand his meaning.

"But what do I know about politics? And what do I care where—wait." The gatekeeper snapped his fingers to emphasize a recollection. "Isn't he the one who claimed to be the Messiah?"

"May we pass?" Andrew carefully pressed.

"Oh. Yes." The gatekeeper chuckled nervously. "Of course." He lifted the crossbeam from the small wooden door built into the massive gate and leaned it against the stone wall. "But remember, once through the needle's eye this night, you won't be allowed through again until daybreak."

"Why not?" Peter challenged.

"Orders handed down by Herod's police and supported by the Roman guard. Not very long ago, either, I might add."

"But why?"

The gatekeeper shrugged his shoulders. "In an effort to tighten the city's security, they decided no more coming and going through any of the city's gates tonight." He winked at Andrew. "A dangerous claim this . . . this Messiah business." He pushed open the small door. "There. You'd better be quick. The Roman guards are surveying the city's gates more frequently this evening. A friend of mine told me they've checked the Fish Gate and the Horse Gate many times already. Otherwise, I'd ask you all to stay and keep me company—and tell me something about this so-called Messiah who's paid the ultimate price for his claim."

Peter patted the gatekeeper on the shoulder. "Yes, well, we'd like to but—"

"No, no. Don't misunderstand my casualness. You must hurry. You, all of you, appear too suspicious. Especially with your wandering about on a night like this. You'd all be arrested on sight, believe me."

Andrew was touched by the gatekeeper's concern. "Thank you, friend, for the warning."

"Bah. You didn't need any warning from me. Your eyes . . . your eyes—damn these Romans, anyway. How many more of us will have to be crucified to satisfy them? Don't answer." He motioned for them to escape. "Go on. Hurry."

As soon as they passed through the needle's eye, the gatekeeper pushed the door closed and dropped the crossbeam into place. The shock of exile and the extreme isolation ahead made them hesitate before the vast outer dark.

"My God," Thaddaeus whispered. "I thought the man would never shut up."

"The road before us leads straight to Galilee," said Peter. "To the right, the road will take us to Jericho."

"And to the left?" Andrew asked, as he surveyed that direction.

"Yes. Our destination. Golgotha."

"Are you sure," Philip called to him from behind. "Are you sure you're alright with this, Peter?"

Peter's back stiffened. "What's alright?"

Philip digested the inverted apology. "I can't experience your pain. I can only experience my own. And—I can forgive you."

Tears rolled down Peter's face. "I could have killed you. Would have if . . . if it hadn't been for Thaddaeus and my brother here."

"Sometimes I believe," Thaddaeus projected lightly, "it would have been easier to remain a disciple of the Baptist—with or without his head."

"Stop being ridiculous," Peter said.

The silence that followed was palpable.

Andrew's unaggressive nature prevented him from confronting his older brother, once again. Despite Peter's exasperating irrationality and hot-tempered nature, Andrew loved him, even liked him. They were very much opposites. Peter was married; Andrew was single and living in his household. Peter was overbearing, and Andrew was an unassuming man, mild, even kindly in temperament. With members of their group, Andrew was quite approachable and, with Jesus, very trusting. He never minded being under Peter's domineering shadow and never minded receiving orders by someone who took charge. He was content to be a follower of Jesus, to whom he was unquestionably devoted, even though he didn't comprehend most of his teaching and, when he did, was usually shocked by its implications.

Thaddaeus, on the other hand, was quite firm but lighthearted when provoked by Peter. He was quiet, steady, and secure in his place among the twelve. Above all, he possessed humor—one of the unappreciated talents within their group. However, he usually chose to blend obscurely into the background when they were in public because he was not a handsome man and because he had frequent, though minor, outbreaks of leprosy.

And then there was Philip. Genuine. Clearminded. But slow at mystical comprehension; Jesus perplexed him. To his favor, he always asked his Master for clarification rather than quietly nursing his doubts, which would otherwise fester into an intolerable war of contradictions within him. This kind of honesty was his greatest strength and contribution among them. "I hope the others are alright—I mean, safe."

"Yes. Safe," Andrew qualified for everybody's sake. "Shall we go?"

Peter began to lead the way to Golgotha. The road was littered with sleeping beggars wrapped in their mantles for warmth and using stones for pillows. The more affluent pilgrims and merchant travelers, who were unable to find a place to stay in the city or at a nearby inn, were nestled in modest little tent camps surrounded by their donkeys and oxen and camels. The camps were cold; the wet weather had prevented any safe use of fire. Small wooden carts, as well as other wheeled vehicles made of latticework debris, were present, although few in number. These conditions were not particularly unusual during the Passover season when an influx of travelers always overcrowded the city of Jerusalem and its surrounding inns, forcing many to take heart and sleep by the roadside when nighttime overtook them and forcing others with lesser means to lament their ill fortune.

The road was wet and slippery, and they stopped along the way to take off their sandals for better footing. Farther along the way, they came upon a water-filled ditch where they stopped again, this time to wash their filthy feet and their mud-caked sandals. This eased some of their misery. They lingered by the ditch, quietly forestalling their visit to Golgotha. And while each man wrestled with his personal ghost, a pack of curious wild dogs maneuvered into their vicinity sniffing the air for any evidence of food.

Thaddaeus saw Peter picking up a rock. "What?"

"Dogs!" Peter threw the rock at one of the lurking silhouettes, but missed.

"Leave them be," Andrew grumbled.

"I hate those snarly, scavenging beasts."

"Every creature snarls when treated badly."

Peter ignored his brother and picked up another stone.

"Golgotha is our destination, remember?" Thaddaeus slipped on his sandals and assisted Philip to his feet. "Fight with dogs all night if you like, but we're leaving."

Andrew turned away from his brother, stepped ahead of Thaddaeus and Philip, and took over leading the way.

Peter dropped the stone and lowered his head in shame as they walked away from him. Unable to express any form of apology, he mutely followed them along the rough country road, into the vacant night, and toward the destination they had been avoiding.

Golgotha was an insignificant hill not far from Jerusalem's walls and, by daylight, could be seen clearly from the road. As soon as they passed a small grove of trees, they encountered a modest incline, which they climbed without effort.

The progression of their perceptions unfolded incrementally: they were appalled by the tangible sensation of agony that lurked in the prevailing darkness; they were stunned by the grudging appearance of three clumsy beams set upon gruesome stakes; they were shocked by the crudeness of an empty cross, then horrified by the wretchedness of the occupied ones when they saw two unconscious men ordained to perish to the bone while nailed to the wood of their destruction.

Peter walked past the shocked figures of Philip and Thaddaeus and Andrew. They were statues, and he was a semiconscious man guided by the need to get close to his Rabbi's instrument of execution.

The Place of the Skull was deserted except for two legionnaires, one asleep and one on guard. Two feeble burning torches smoking toward extinguishment were impaled haphazardly into the wet ground, and one oil lamp protected by an enclosed hand carrying lantern sat near the legionnaires. The on-duty soldier seemed amused by the arrival of four distraught spectators, even grateful to have a new drama unfold before him to break his monotonous watch. It was obvious that he wasn't about to interrupt their visit, as long as they did not cause any trouble.

Peter fell to his knees and hugged the front of the cross's thick, vertical stake. Above him loomed the protruding support peg used to help keep the crucified in place in the most uncomfortable manner between the legs. To increase the degradation, the above peg was sculpted into a grotesque, circumcised penis. Peter pressed his forehead against the stake and began to sob. Then he kissed the wood several times before he hugged the stake to near convulsion.

Andrew responded in the way all brothers do. "For heaven's sake, Peter, get a hold of yourself. Remember, death is not the end."

"Don't quote our Master to me! I know what he said. I know what he said!"

Thaddaeus placed a reassuring hand upon Andrew's shoulder. "Leave him alone. Let him cry. There's nothing that can be done for him. As Philip said, we can only experience our own pain."

Andrew nodded. "Right." He gazed blankly at Philip. "You're right, my friend."

Philip directed their attention to the head of the cross. "Andrew, look." He pointed upward with greater emphasis. "You too, Thaddaeus."

Together, they read it aloud. "Jesus of Nazareth, King of the Jews."

"Those despicable Romans." Thaddaeus spat on the ground. "They'll say and do anything to maintain their power over us."

Philip shuddered. Andrew closed his eyes from the sadness. And for a few moments, they mourned with the same intensity as Peter, whose arms remained wrapped tightly around the cross's stake, while his face remained pressed obliviously against the wood. Then

Philip shook himself out of his misery and approached Andrew with a lighter determination. "Remember the time I didn't know what to do with those pagan Greeks who wanted to meet our Master?"

Andrew grinned. "I remember."

"You were right when you assured me that Jesus would speak to those gentiles. He wanted everybody to benefit by his word. I was so stupid."

"Be gentle with yourself, as well," Andrew cautioned. "He chose you, remember? He chose all of us. Who among us have ever been able to understand even a tenth of his radical ideas?"

"That's right," Thaddaeus interjected. "He was the Messiah . . . wasn't he?"

Andrew was infected by Thaddaeus's doubtful tone. "Well . . . yes. Of course."

"The Messiah," Philip declared. "Say it. The Messiah."

They heard a huge groan from above and to the right, followed by a deep and harsh croak of a single word. "What!" Then another. "What?!" The hairy brutish man to the right lifted his head from unconsciousness as he opened his eyes. He heard Peter sobbing. "Who is that? Get away, damn you! A curse on all of you for awakening me into this pain!"

Andrew approached him. "We're . . . we're sorry we brought you back to your agony."

"Sorry! Sorry is not enough!" He tried to spit at Andrew, but his throat was too dry. "What are you doing here?"

"We came . . . we came, we hoped, to see something of our Master."

"Ha! You mean that something lunatic they've already taken down?"

Andrew backed away from the poor, miserable wretch in order to break communications with him. He glanced at the guard, then took several steps in his direction.

"What are you doing?" Philip whispered vehemently.

"I have an idea."

"What. What?"

"Stay there."

Andrew cautiously approached the guard, who was fascinated by what he was witnessing. "Sir. I . . . I have nothing to offer you but, but gratitude." He hesitated.

"Yes?" The legionnaire revealed his curiosity by leaning against his pilum. "Go on."

"Would it be possible, I mean, could you allow me to provide something to quench that man's thirst?"

"I could. What for?" Again, Andrew hesitated. "I said what for?"

Andrew became tongue-tied. "I . . . I—"

"Don't be afraid. I'll not hurt you as long as you amuse me. Over there is a jar of posca. And beside it there's a sponge tied to a rod long enough to reach his mouth. Use it to quench his thirst. Azriel wasn't a bad sort, really. Of the three, he's the one I'd choose to feel sorry for."

"Azriel, you say?"

"That's him. A thief and a murderer. Like his young companion over there."

Andrew dared another question. "And his name?"

"Nikos. A boy, really. And under the influence of someone who got him crucified."

"You mean, Azriel."

"Who else? Go on, now. Entertain me before I lose my patience."

Thaddaeus accosted Andrew beside the jar of posca. "Is this . . . is this wise?"

"We're here to find out what happened to our Master, aren't we?" Andrew scrutinized Azriel. "That man was present at his death."

"He's a criminal."

"He," Andrew glanced at Nikos, "they, shared in his suffering. Can you understand that? They were more than present." He grabbed the jar by its mouth as he snatched the rod by the neck near the attached sponge. "Follow me."

Philip was standing near Azriel. "Can I help?"

"Just listen." Andrew set the jar down, shook the sponge clean of surface dirt, and immersed it into the dark red liquid. "This posca smells more like vinegar than wine."

None of this had escaped Azriel's attention. His eyes were wide with anticipation.

Philip studied Azriel's wretched condition. The man trembled with constant pain. His arms were extended and tied along the length of a crossbeam and nailed at the wrists into the wood. His body sat heavily on a thick peg protruding from the stake, which was wedged between his legs. The excruciating position seemed to crush his scrotum underneath his weight. His right leg was nailed at the ankle to the side of the stake noticeably higher than the left leg, also nailed to the wood. The lingering odor of excrement, which came from the diarrhea-coated support peg and the lower portion of the stake, emphasized the naked humiliation this man was suffering.

"Haven't you ever seen a crucified man before?" Philip was startled by Azriel's direct address. "That's right. I'm talking to you."

"No."

"Hey. You two. Over there. Will you hurry up with that damn wine before that guard changes his mind?"

Andrew pulled the heavily soaked sponge out of the jar, then carefully maneuvered it up to Azriel by its attached rod. Azriel gnawed on the sponge like a wild beast when Andrew pressed the sponge against his lips. Wine dripped along his face and neck and chest, and drops spattered to the ground. Andrew didn't attempt to pull it away until he was sure Azriel would permit it. When he finally lowered the rod, Azriel's glazed eyes accented the reverie in his face. Andrew didn't dare disturb Azriel's single moment of comfort.

While Andrew continued to study Azriel with Philip, Thaddaeus timidly meandered toward the other poor creature and scrutinized him with great sympathy. "This one appears to be dead."

"The lucky bastard!" Azriel croaked. Then he laughed. "The poor young idiot thinks he's gone to heaven with that clown they took down. Ha!"

Thaddaeus turned to him excitedly. "What was that?" He caught Andrew and Philip's eager glances. "What did he say to the boy?"

"He promised," Azriel shouted facetiously. "Before he died, he promised he would take the boy with him to heaven this day."

"This . . . very . . . day?" Thaddaeus repeated.

Even Peter was dumbfounded enough to release his embrace from his Master's stake, twist around on his knees, and look up at Azriel with the rest of them. "This is monstrous."

"This is justice!" Azriel teased cruelly. "Roman justice!"

Peter looked at Nikos. "Our Master said that to him?"

"Master! Ha! Mad man, you mean!"

"Please, don't say that."

"Bah. Your Master and that little shit over there have gone to heaven. And you're still here. What do you think of that? Ha!" Azriel choked and gurgled with pain and suffocation and cruelty. "More wine."

Andrew quickly recharged the sponge by immersing it into the posca, then he brought it up to Azriel's eager face.

Azriel bit into the sponge less violently and sucked on it with increased care to get more wine into him. There was no hope of getting drunk, but the relief he derived from his broken thirst left him ecstatic.

"How did he die?" Peter demanded without showing him pity. He stood up.

Andrew pulled the sponge away from him. "My brother asked you a question."

"Go to hell!" Azriel was prepared to fight, even at the hour of his death.

"Then . . . then I'm asking you," Andrew said carefully. "You owe me nothing."

"I know that!"

"But I'd . . . we'd like to know. Please."

Azriel considered the request for a very long time. "He died—with dignity. I have to admit that much. Your luna—your leader, died with great dignity. I'll give him that much. Wine."

Andrew dipped the sponge into the jar and brought the drenched sponge to Azriel's insatiable mouth again. The disciples watched the dying man with morbid fascination and genuine pity. They were mesmerized into a moment of introspection:

This was the reason why they ran away and hid like vermin. This is why they denied their allegiance and swore against him at his final hours. This is what reduced them to cowards and brought them to shame.

"That's enough posca for him," the legionnaire commanded. He'd grown bored with them.

The loss of his only comfort launched Azriel into another tirade. "So, you want to know about your leader, the King of the Jews? Ha! If you hadn't been cowards to the core, you wouldn't have been late. Now you have to settle with me! I'm your leader. Look! Look at your Messiah!" Azriel cackled insanely with deep cruelty. "Get away from me, you lice! The lot of you together wouldn't make one good thief! Go on, I say. You're no longer useful to me. Get out. You're not men enough to watch me die!"

Andrew placed the rod on the ground by leaning it on top of the jar with the sponge hooked into its mouth. Then he joined the others and shambled away from Azriel in disgrace. Once again, Golgotha had taken more than it had given.

They walked quietly through a grove of trees, then into the open countryside where they wandered aimlessly through the thick evening until they came to a free-standing, two-story structure just off the road. They circled around the building in search of a dry place to sit out the night and discovered, to their horror, Judas hanging by his neck from a rafter under the structure's crude portico.

Andrew gasped. "My God!"

Peter approached the dangling body in the same way Andrew had approached Azriel. He reached out and touched him, then pulled back his hand as if he'd touched a hot iron. "He's dead." Peter studied Judas's tragic figure.

The belt that Judas used for a noose cut deeply into his neck and caused his tongue to protrude grotesquely out of his gaping mouth. Strands of greasy hair crisscrossed his battered face. And from head to foot, he was stained with blood and mud and excrement. He smelled like sewage.

"His tongue is blue," Philip commented without thought.

"Yes." Peter approached a large clay pot. "He must have kicked this pot out from under himself." He turned the pot right side up and stared at it. "Himself. Whoever that was."

They heard someone from inside the structure remove the crossbar from the door leading into the portico. A bareheaded woman stepped outside as soon as the door was opened. "You didn't sound like legionnaires." She noticed Thaddaeus's sympathetic expression before he tore his gaze from Judas's remains. "You knew this man?"

"He . . . he was one of us," Thaddaeus said.

"But not of Ganto's band," she qualified.

"Ganto."

"No, of course not." She studied them with a measure of disdain. "You must be the devoted followers of the other one."

"Not . . . not, quite so devoted." Thaddaeus pretended to smooth the ground in front of him with the bottom of his right foot. "Jesus was our Master."

"Yes, yes." She bit her lip inquisitively. "You were there, at Golgotha?"

"Yes."

"No."

She looked at Thaddaeus, then Peter. "Well then, which is it? There or not there?"

"There," Thaddaeus insisted, "after it was over."

"You mean—"

"Our Master was dead and gone by the time we got there."

"That's right. That's right," Peter said defensively. "We just came from Golgotha."

She squeezed and twisted the loose portion of her tunic above her breast with her anxious fist. "And the others?"

"The others? What about them?"

"One of them was my man."

The disciples cringed.

Andrew approached her with sympathy. "Would he have been the older one?"

"Of course. Azriel."

"And you're?—"

"Dinah. His woman."

"I see."

The disciples shared numerous glances at one another.

She caught their furtive exchanges. "What?"

"He's a hard man," Andrew said.

"Then . . . then he's still alive?"

"I'm afraid so."

"And with all his senses," Thaddaeus added.

"My God." Dinah's voice hardened. "If there is a God. How does he look?"

"Wretched," Thaddaeus offered impotently.

"That's no description."

The four of them remained silent.

Dinah went to her doorway, reached inside the opening, and retrieved her mantle. "You're not even men enough to describe what you've seen. What kind of men are you? And what kind of leader was this Rabbi of yours who wouldn't even fight to save his own life?" She shut her tavern door and stormed through them. "Out of my way, you cowards." She pushed Andrew aside and muttered to herself as if the disciples weren't present. "I'm coming, Azriel. Curse at me all you want. But I'm not going to leave you alone any longer. I hope my presence gives you some kind of comfort, even if cursing at me can help you forget some of your pain." She stopped, suddenly, peered at Judas, then threw a sharp glance at them. "Do something with him. I don't want him here when I return."

The disciples watched her disappear into the countryside's darkness in silence.

"At least she's in time," Peter said.

"There you go again." Andrew walked away from Peter, filled with exasperation. "All you want to hear is words of forgiveness. All you want is—"

"Redemption! Yes! Yes. *Yes*." Peter fell to his hands and knees and sobbed.

Thaddaeus quietly knelt beside him in pity and placed a consoling hand on Peter's trembling back.

"I've forgotten how to pray," Peter said.

"I don't think I ever knew how."

"I refuse to pray," Philip confessed. "I won't . . . I won't be a hypocrite."

"Then help me take Judas down." Andrew was standing within reach of the body. "I can't bear looking at him in this condition any longer."

Philip came to Andrew's assistance, but winced as soon as he reached up to catch hold of Judas.

Andrew placed a concerned hand on Philip's closest forearm. "Wait. Don't you dare. I forgot about your injury."

"That's alright. I want to help."

"I know, I know. But I don't want you to start bleeding again. Please. Stand over there. Thaddaeus can help, instead."

Thaddaeus left Peter where he was to assist Andrew. He took hold of Judas's legs after Andrew rolled the large pot close enough for him to step onto it and untie the belt from the rafter. In the meantime, Philip approached Peter from behind, knelt beside him in Thaddaeus's place, and pressed a sympathetic hand on his colleague's shoulder.

Lowering Judas's body with care required tremendous effort.

As a group, they were emotionally exhausted. Peter and Philip were kneeling side by side nearly holding their breaths, while Andrew and Thaddaeus sat near Judas's body, panting softly. Nobody wanted to speak. The bleak night continued without stars in the sky.

Andrew removed the noose from Judas's neck. "We can't stay here all night." Nobody responded. "And we can't leave Judas here."

"He's no longer with us," Thaddaeus said flatly.

"He never was one of us." Peter stood up. "The convert."

"Peter!" Andrew shot up to his feet as well. "Damn. You amaze me."

"Our Master knew what he was up to."

"Yes. And he did not judge him. So, why should we?"

Peter scowled at Judas. "That's not a good justification."

"I don't need one," Andrew retorted. "Our Master has already forgiven him. Just as he forgave you, remember? He said he prayed for you. He prayed that your faith wouldn't fail. In fact, he prayed for all of us.

Because he knew. He knew our strength and conviction would not withstand the true test. We abandoned him. We. And your denial, well, you spoke for all of us."

"Cold comfort," Peter muttered.

"I don't think his forgiveness is about comfort. Anyway, it's done. With or without your understanding."

"I don't believe that!"

"And with or without your belief!" Andrew stood nose to nose with his brother, reflecting the same heat of anger. "Who are we to act superior? And what do we know about Judas's deeds other than what's been rumored? Hearsay means nothing." His anger deflated as he turned away from Peter. He continued speaking with an uncharacteristic detachment. "Like I said, our Master has forgiven him—all of us—without our asking. It is done. It's done."

Peter inhaled and exhaled deeply. "I'm nothing. Really, really nothing. Where shall we take him?"

"Among the trees, I suppose." Andrew pointed to a distant grove that remained perceptible to them because they had traveled through them earlier. "Perhaps in there. What do you think?"

"Maybe we can find a deep enough hollow and cover him with leaves."

"Yes. We'll bury him properly later."

Peter made sure that Philip and Thaddaeus had been listening. "Everybody agree?" Peter interpreted their continued silence for a yes. "Good. Help me lift him to my shoulders."

"Let me share some of the burden," Andrew said.

"No, no. I'm strong enough to carry him alone."

"But—"

"It'll be easier for me, really. Really, I . . . I don't need to share this burden."

"Yes. Alright."

They assisted Peter in mounting Judas over his right shoulder. He tested the weight with a couple of steps. "Good. Let's go."

Andrew ran in front of his brother to lead the way, Thaddaeus positioned himself behind Peter just in case he stumbled, and Philip managed his injury alone as he plodded along.

The informal funeral procession labored through the darkness toward their destination. They were on the edge of complete physical exhaustion: Peter's breathing could be heard, and Thaddaeus was stumbling too often; Philip was lagging behind, and Andrew was simply numb. The grove's distance seemed longer on their return trip.

The gloom deepened when they finally pierced the edge of the grove. They proceeded under the influence of these trees and fallen debris, which made night travel more difficult. Peter stumbled and regained his balance several times after going a short distance. Even after their progress was reduced to a crawl, this did not prevent Peter from stepping into a small hole that Andrew missed seeing. He tumbled to his right, the side burdened by Judas's weight. It was a hard-hitting fall that caused Peter to yelp with surprise, then grunt helplessly upon impact. Judas's body rolled straight down a hill and, after being deflected into another direction by an obstruction, the body stopped abruptly at the bottom of the depression.

Andrew hurried alongside Peter. "Are you alright?"

Peter was panting too heavily to complete a full phrase. "Wind. Lost. Wind." His wheezing overtook him. "Sorry."

Andrew remained at his side while Thaddaeus and Philip went to retrieve Judas's body.

"Woe. Look at this, Philip."

"What is it?"

Andrew heard Philip gasp. "What's happened?" Peter's heavy breathing eased up with curiosity and, by tapping his hand against his brother's leg, he encouraged Andrew to inquire once again. "What's going on?"

"It's Judas," Philip answered. "He's . . . he's torn open at the gut. His insides, they're . . . they're all spilled out."

"Help me up, Andrew. Please."

Andrew assisted Peter to his feet and together they shambled down the hill to join the others.

"That jagged timber impaled on the ground," Thaddaeus said, still crouched beside Judas's body. "See it? It's raised on a dangerous angle."

"That must have been the cause," Philip added superfluously.

"Of course it was," Peter retorted. "Can't you see that piece of Judas still hooked to it?"

Andrew thumped his brother's side with his elbow.

Peter winced. "I'm sorry."

"Not to me."

"I'm sorry, Philip."

"Forget it."

Thaddaeus stood up. "Seems to me, we should bury him where he's at."

"That's sensible," Andrew said. "Let's do it."

Thaddaeus crouched beside Judas again, rolled him on his back, and did his best to push Judas's internal organs back inside the abdominal cavity, while the others gathered leaves and fallen debris to use as ground cover over Judas. Thaddaeus managed to keep Judas's internal organs loosely in place by tying the front of Judas's torn tunic securely over the sight. He arranged Judas's hands and feet in the customary manner. Then he tore a piece of his own tunic, at the lowest end, and placed it over Judas's face. "That's the best I can do for you, my friend."

"Don't worry," Philip said, standing beside Thaddaeus with the last armful of debris he intended to gather. "It's a temporary burial."

"Right. I hope so."

"Let's get started."

Andrew and Peter continued gathering, while Thaddaeus and Philip covered the body. They worked quietly and reverently until the task was complete. Then they assembled around the sight to rest and remember.

The ground was drier and more comfortable with the extra layer of ground cover beneath them. And with several nearby trees, the surroundings felt more like a camp. Their communal exhale was the first moment of well-being they had experienced that night.

Thaddaeus and Peter were stretched out on the ground, Andrew and Philip sat leaning against a tree.

Thaddaeus gently touched Philip with his foot. "Remember that time we had that huge fight on the outskirts of—what was the name of that village?"

"Who knows. It doesn't matter." Philip chuckled. "But I remember that argument you had with Judas. He really infuriated you that afternoon."

"I'll say." Thaddaeus frowned. "You know, he had a lot on his shoulders. I certainly wouldn't have wanted the burden of carrying the purse or the responsibility of having to get us fed each day. I should have given him more credit."

"Don't start thinking like Andrew's brother over there."

Peter lifted his head with resentment. "What?"

"Go back to sleep."

"I wasn't asleep." Peter sulked quietly, while Thaddaeus and Philip continued their recollection.

"If I remember correctly," Philip said, "you're the one who started that argument."

"Right," Thaddaeus said with embarrassment. "And to think, I called him the violent one."

"Names. It's never good calling people names."

"Like convert?"

"He resented you for that."

"I know."

"He should've gotten more of our respect."

"Please. Enough. You've always defended Judas."

"That's because Philip is the only one among us who wasn't jealous of him," Andrew interjected.

"Jealous!"

"Sure. I'm just as guilty. I remember: our Master quietly favored Judas in some hidden and untouchable manner."

"Jesus favored me!" Peter declared childishly.

Andrew scowled at his brother. "Yes, yes. In words. Loudly, even. But in words. For *your* benefit. For *our* display. But with Judas, with Judas, well: there was this . . . this quiet understanding. And with it, always a gentle restlessness between them. Quite frankly, I believe they were necessary for each other."

Peter sat up, crossed his arms against his chest, and remained deeply sullen within his forced silence.

Thaddaeus nudged Philip. "And I remember how confused you looked when our Master told us to feed that hungry crowd near Tiberias after he had spent the day teaching them."

"Oh, God." Philip blushed. "There were thousands of hungry mouths, remember?"

"Do I."

"But Judas and . . . and Andrew here, never had a moment of doubt when it really counted."

"Sure I did," Andrew protested.

"No. I don't remember a single doubt uttered from you. Not one objection. You simply went among the crowd and found that boy who had five barley loaves and a couple of fish." Philip forced eye contact with Peter. "Now that scared me." The remark caught them all off guard. Even Peter had to laugh. "Think of it. What were we expected to do with five loaves and two fishes among so many hungry mouths? To tell you the truth, I was expecting a riot."

"But he did it, didn't he," Andrew said, taking over the story.

Thaddaeus whistled with amazement. "Damn if it didn't look like magician's work."

"But it wasn't," Andrew insisted. "And we all know that." He waited until everybody agreed. "And believe me when I say this, it was Judas's example that I followed. It was he who went into the crowd first to seek the food our Lord requested. But it just happened to be me who found the boy."

"Is that how it happened?" Peter asked.

"Yes, big brother." Andrew gazed at the mound of debris and, in so doing, directed the others to do the same. "Judas had a deep trust, an awareness, that our Master had control over the laws of nature."

"Then what happened to him?" Thaddaeus was deeply perplexed. "And why did he seem so tense and confused and irritated all the time?"

"Because . . . because we never helped him or fully trusted him or ever included him into our personal fold."

"That was no reason to kill himself, Andrew."

"No, but when I saw him kiss our Master just before his arrest—"

"I saw that," Thaddaeus interjected enthusiastically.

Philip's furtive glance induced Peter to remain silent.

"I believe," Andrew continued, "I believe Judas was involved in hidden matters, which had grown beyond his control—"

"And beyond our Master's control, as well?" Thaddaeus's eyes bulged. "Preposterous!"

"Perhaps. Perhaps not. In any case, suicide is not a coward's way out. Suicide—"

"Is the end."

"Or . . . or his only way to the Kingdom of Heaven."

"That's lunacy!" Peter finally managed to say.

"Or jealousy?" Andrew challenged.

Peter was stunned. He looked at Philip, who had remained quiet. Peter seemed to shrink before him. He lowered his head. "You're right, Andrew. You're right. Aside from Philip here, I believe we, and all the rest of us, were jealous of Judas. Jealous." Peter smashed his right fist into the palm of his left hand. "Damn. I admit it. I admit it, alright?"

Andrew smiled proudly at his brother for the first time since Jesus' arrest. They had made Judas human again. And if not fully redeemed in their eyes, certainly by God's—and certainly forgiven in their hearts. But this conclusion, along with his sibling pride, was tarnished by his brother's persistent and destructive sense of guilt.

"But only the dead can be forgiven," Peter said. "What about us? What about me?"

"I've told you, already," Andrew said with clear exasperation. "It is done. Our Master has forgiven you. Him. Me. Us." He searched his brother's eyes. "Where is your faith? Where is your faith?"

"In the pit of my stomach—churning. In the seat of my heart—crying. In the caverns of my mind—hiding." Peter exhaled into the calmness of a madman. "I am lost. I am lost. There's no hope."

"Then I can't help you." Andrew leaned heavily

against the tree and closed his eyes. "I'm tired. I'm too tired to go on."

Andrew was unaware that he had spoken for all of them. His declared resignation was infectious. Each man, in his own method, succumbed to a torpor state: neither asleep nor awake, alive nor dead. Their vacant stares were not a result of deep internal reflections or long probing projections into the night. Their vacancy was a true emptiness waiting to be filled up by something, anything; perhaps not by a substance, but by an event, instead—an event as simple as daybreak.

Philip was the only one who stayed awake. His head buzzed with exhaustion, and he was afraid. The wound to his side was nagging him with sharp pain, and he felt hot despite the cold and wet conditions. He couldn't get comfortable, and the frequent shifting of positions aggravated his injury and intensified his concern.

The glow of dawn was on the horizon, and the world was returning to the light. Philip studied a bird perched on a tree branch for an undetermined period of time. When it flew away and broke his concentration, he was surprised to discover Andrew sitting up.

"I can't believe we fell asleep."

"The city's gate should be opened by now." Philip's voice was hoarse and weak.

Andrew grimaced with concern. He stood up and stretched, then hobbled over to Philip, looking as if he had arthritis in all his joints. He placed the back of his right hand against Philip's forehead. "You're burning up."

"I don't feel good, either."

"You're as white as a ghost."

"All I need is to get into a dry tunic and find a nice warm place to sleep. I'll be alright, then."

"Sure, sure, dry and warm is all you need." Andrew shuffled over to his brother and nudged him on his side with his foot. "Wake up."

Peter jerked up into a sitting position. "What. What? I wasn't asleep." He shook his head. "I just dozed off for a minute."

"Sure you did." Andrew turned away from him, crouched beside Thaddaeus, and gave him a gentle shake. "Time to get up."

Thaddaeus rolled toward him. "Good morning."

"What's good about it?" Peter grumbled.

"And good morning to you, too." Thaddaeus sat up. "Did you get any sleep?"

"Some." Andrew pointed to Philip. "But he didn't. He's as hot as red-iron with fever. I'm afraid to look at his wound."

"Infection?"

"I hope not."

"Let's go see."

Thaddaeus stood up, shook off some of the debris clinging to his hair and tunic, and accompanied Andrew to inspect Philip's condition.

Philip released a ragged cough as he tried to wave them away. "Please, don't burden me with your worry."

Thaddaeus grabbed Andrew by the arm before he

was able to crouch beside Philip. "Wait. Look. Some-one's coming."

Peter stood up and studied the approaching figure. "I know that gait." He squinted harder. "Isn't that?—I think that's my son."

The boy called out to him. "Father? Father. Is that you?"

"Over here, boy. Come on. Over here." As he hurried to reach Peter, relief could be seen on the boy's face. "What are you doing out here, son?"

The boy was confused by his father's question. "I . . . I was sent. Mother sent me out to find you. She's been worried all night."

"Is everybody safe?"

The boy nodded his head, then counteracted it with a shrug. "So far. Everybody is not accounted for, yet." The boy hesitated before venturing his own question. "Where . . . where have you all been, Father?"

Peter looked away, too embarrassed to answer him.

"He's been in hiding," Philip said, not realizing he was taking revenge. "Hiding with the rest of us."

The boy frowned. "Oh. Mother's not going to be happy about that."

"Who's asked you, boy?"

Andrew held his temper. And Thaddaeus knew better than to step between father and son.

The boy cowered under Peter's wrath. "I'm sorry, Father. I . . . I didn't mean to make you angry." The boy was on the verge of tears. It was evident that he hadn't slept all night. "It's been an awful night. I've never seen the women cry so much."

"And you? Have you managed to hold back your tears?"

The boy proudly straightened up. "Most of the time." He bit his lip thoughtfully. "But that was impossible to do when . . . when—" the boy almost broke into tears, but he managed to shudder beyond the moment. He blinked his eyes steadily.

"Well?" Peter demanded.

"When our Master was being crucified."

Andrew's eyes widened. "You were there?"

"Yes, Uncle."

Peter glanced at his brother, Andrew, with increased guilt and horror. "Even my boy had greater strength than I during the crucial hours."

The boy was confused by his father's remark. He wanted to say something to comfort him, but he was afraid.

Andrew ignored his self-pitying brother. "Tell me, Eli. Tell me what you saw." He glanced at Thaddaeus, then Philip. Both men were filled with the desire to live through the event they had missed, forever. "Tell us what happened."

"Mother kept covering my eyes as she wept, but I saw, I saw—" The boy had to check his emotions, once again. "I'm sorry, it's difficult. I . . . I cried when they drove the nails into his body."

Andrew glared at Peter to insure that the boy would be allowed to regain his composure unmolested by his father's temper. In fact, he approached Eli and encouraged him to sit down. The others sat down in turn and, in so doing, diffused some of the tension and sorrow. "Have you eaten anything lately?"

Eli shook his head. "Not much." He gazed up at his uncle. "I couldn't." He placed a hand on his stomach for emphasis. "It feels all knotted up inside. I don't think I'll ever be hungry again."

Andrew sat beside the boy and embraced him by laying a comforting arm across the boy's slender shoulders. Then he patiently waited for Eli to gather his thoughts. The others remained quietly wrapped with anticipation, afraid to say anything that would disturb the boy's ability to narrate his story.

They waited forbearingly. Breathlessly. Then impatiently.

The boy studied them. Submissively. Then he spoke.

"When the storm descended upon us, we became frightened. Not until then. He was alive, until then, you see?" Eli cast his eyes downward. "But with the storm, came the emptiness of his presence. His death, it . . . it changed everything. On Golgotha's mound, lightning struck everywhere. And that wind, the wind, it . . . it wouldn't have been so bad if it hadn't been for the rain that hurt my face like sand. It was awful. Even the legionnaires panicked and almost unsheathed their swords against us; they thought we had something to do with . . . with these . . . these earth changes—that's it! That's why it was so frightening. It wasn't mere weather we were experiencing. It was earth changes." The boy was reliving the story as he spoke. "The legionnaires finally realized that these conditions were beyond our understanding as well. So, they stood fast and threw their cloaks over their heads and across their faces for protection while the rest of us tried to run from this unnatural, this . . . this unleashed power." Eli shrugged his shoulders. "I don't know why we ran; there was no place to go, no place to get away from it. But who thinks when they are suffocating with fear? Who thinks when the world is coming to an end?" He glanced at Andrew, then looked away. "I held onto Mother's girdle and together we trampled upon the trembling earth in the direction of the mob—down the hill and into the strange darkness." Eli smiled at himself. "Silly. We sought refuge by running back to the city where everybody else was huddling inside their leaking homes—that is, if they had the sense to stay home. Anyway, everybody got separated from each other, but I held onto Mother. Eventually, we found our way back to safety and, throughout the night, a few others showed up at Aaron's door as well. Later, we got word from Naomi, she was the last of us to get back safely, that his Mother and Mary of Magdala had stayed behind and beyond the storm. That's how we knew about his burial. Naomi was there. And after they placed him in the tomb, she volunteered to find us in order to ease our sorrow. But I don't know about my own sorrow's ease." The boy paused momentarily to gather his thoughts, but the men became too impatient to allow this.

"Tell us more about what happened after they took him down from the cross," said Philip. "Tell us how this burial had come to happen."

"Some men took him down."

"His name, son, his name!"

70

The boy reached into his memory. "Joseph, I think. Joseph, yes."

"Joseph who?"

"Of . . . of Arimathea, that's it."

"And?"

"Well, he and his servants took him down from the cross and wrapped him in linen."

"Was he taken to a good place of rest?" Andrew prompted.

"Yes. I heard he was buried in a tomb made of rock where no one had ever yet been laid."

"Where? Where!"

"His mother and Mary and . . . and Naomi! You'll have to ask them, Father."

"Bah! How was this possible?" Peter ranted with exasperation. "Who is this man who was able to rescue a crucified body from the wild dogs and carrion birds?"

"And before the Sabbath, as well," Thaddaeus agreed.

The boy coughed.

"If you know anything, son, tell us."

The boy looked at Andrew to regain his confidence. "I overheard he was a high ranking counselor in Judea."

"Hmm. Never heard of him."

"Naomi overheard him say that he'd wished he knew more about our Rabbi's Kingdom of God."

Andrew looked at Peter. "A follower. One of us."

"It certainly seems so."

"And one who possesses much influence."

"Yes." Peter scratched his face. "Then why didn't

he come forward sooner and use his influence on our Master's behalf?"

"Perhaps he was afraid," Philip suggested.

Andrew threw a harsh glance at Philip. "Yes. He probably did hear our Master speak. But in secret."

"But . . . but why wait until now to . . . to—"

"Don't ask for reasons, my brother. Don't ask." Andrew caressed the boy gently. "Anything more, Eli?"

"Apparently, this Joseph took counsel with another man."

"What? Where?"

"At the tomb."

"Spit it out, son!"

Eli averted his eyes from his father's. "His name was Nicodemus. And I was told that he brought many spices, along with a concoction of aloe and myrrh."

"Then his body really was well prepared for burial," Philip said.

"At least. At least he was treated better in death," Thaddaeus added.

"At least, at least." Peter waved his arms with exasperation and began to rave. "Dead and buried and—"

"Let your son finish his story!" Andrew regarded the boy gravely, but spoke gently to him. "Tell me, my young nephew, how?—no, I mean—" He didn't know what to ask first. "When did he die?"

"I don't know the hour. I was simply there when Jesus lifted his voice and said, *'Father, into your hands I commend my spirit.'* " The boy's lips trembled. "Then he lowered his poor battered head and . . . and he was gone. He was gone! A streak of lightning cut the sky in two, right on that moment, and forced everybody to look away: first, in fear, then in shame. I . . . I don't know why, exactly, the shame. Had I not felt the emotion myself and the ground trembling beneath me, I wouldn't have understood it." His face became twisted with confusion. "But I didn't understand it. I still don't. And I was there." Again, the boy's lips trembled for self-control. "He cried out only one time. Unlike the other two who cried and cursed throughout their suffering the entire time they were conscious, the poor devils. Even his one cry was, in a way, self-inflicted." His voice became hollow sounding. "It was the only moment of complete emptiness I'd ever experienced from him." He drew a clean breath. "As impossible as this may sound, it made me lose and reinforce my hope at the same time. That's not possible, you might think; that's not possible, I know. But it's true. I was there. It's true. I heard it. True. I felt it. *My God, my God, why have you forsaken me!*' Then I heard someone say something about Elias, but I was too shattered to comprehend anything else, just then." He glanced at Peter. "Mother went to her knees at that moment. In fact, we all did. Funny, how I suddenly remember that. I was too detached from myself to feel my body, to remember, until now that I—we—went to our knees sobbing helplessly first, before we ran." The boy bravely wiped the two streaks of tears from his face. "He forgave us, you know. He forgave everybody. Even as the Roman guards cast lots for his garments. I heard him. He said: *'Father, forgive them, for they do not know what they are doing.'* I heard him. I was there." He shook his head somberly; his eyes reflected wonder. "How was he able to do that with his body so torn and beaten?" Eli shifted uneasily to the image he recollected. "His face was streaked with the blood of his wounds caused by that horrible crown of thorns on his head."

The men stirred uneasily after hearing about this cruel indignation. Andrew involuntarily dropped his arm from the boy's shoulders. Philip pressed a feverish hand against his wound. Thaddaeus covered his eyes with the inner elbow joint of his left arm. Peter stood up and strode several steps away from the group in a ludicrous attempt to prevent himself from hearing anymore of the boy's report.

"A crown, you say?"

The edge of the boy's mouth twitched. "Yes. A plait of sharp thorns, Uncle, crudely fashioned into a tight wreath."

"Making him the King of the Jews," Thaddaeus whispered.

The boy was startled by the remark.

Peter stomped back among them. "You'd have thought the placard was enough! Damn their eyes!" He circled among them like a heated animal in search of a kill. His rage flattened when he discovered he was being ignored.

Andrew steadied the boy with a tender gaze. "Are you able to go on?"

"Yes." Eli swallowed hard. "Anywhere you looked, his body had been violated. Fingernails were torn from his hands. Skin was shredded off his back. Spikes were driven into his wrists and ankles. Even his genitals were crushed against a support peg for all to see. Horrible. His nakedness was horrible." The boy licked his lips. He rubbed his dry mouth with his left hand. "Despite all of that, he found the strength to make a promise." Amazement illuminated the boy's eyes. "He actually made a promise to one of those two criminals hanging on the wood beside him. An ordinary criminal." Eli stared into the darkness. "I wish . . . I wish I'd been brave enough to trade places with him."

"You mean, with Jesus?" Andrew carefully inserted.

"No." The boy's tone became shrill. "No. With the younger one on the cross!" He bit his lip to suppress his panic. "I know it doesn't make any sense."

Andrew patted the boy's thigh. "That's alright. You don't have to be sensible. Go on, if you can."

"Well . . . if you'd have heard his—" Eli searched for clarity within himself. "He spoke directly to our Master in a manner I'd never heard anyone speak to him before. The words. The words weren't as important as the stripped tone in his voice. There was hope. No. There was certainty—that's it. It was the bare certainty I heard when he said to our Master: 'Lord, remember me when you enter into your Kingdom'," Eli laughed softly, almost hysterically. "Then our Master said, *Amen, amen I say to you, this day you will be with me in paradise.*' In paradise, he said to him. Not to me. Not to any of us who loved him and stood before him trembling. But to a criminal not much older than myself. To a nobody. To less than nobody. To less than me." The boy could not go on. He was exhausted by the telling of his emotions.

His insensitive father, however, demanded more from him. "What about men? Were there any of our men among you?"

The boy squirmed in place and avoided his father's eyes. "None. None but John."

"How did you know when it was time to go to Golgotha?" Andrew inquired.

"We . . . we followed the increasing crowd."

"Were you able to catch a glimpse of him, then?"

"Yes. Especially when he fell." Eli's eyes darted from side to side expecting to be interrupted by his father, but he wasn't. "By the time we caught up to the procession, the growing crowd behind him almost kept us separated. But Mother was fiercely determined. We managed to reach the grieving women who were able to stay close to him the entire time." The boy inhaled on the verge of tears, then exhaled on real tears. "His humiliation was constant. Constant."

"Yes. Yes, we understand," Andrew said.

"No. No! You can't know. Not unless you saw."

"But we saw the placard on his empty cross."

"And?" The boy averted his eyes. "I see."

A long and uncomfortable silence followed. Everybody avoided each other's eyes. Philip saved them with a ragged cough, which drew attention to his declining condition.

"Is he alright?" the boy asked.

"No," Peter said.

"Should I run back to Aaron's and bring back some food and drink?"

"Don't be stupid, boy," Peter snapped. "Can't you see he needs the care of women?"

"Peter!" Andrew glared at his brother, who shrank in disgrace. Andrew placed a friendly hand on Eli's head and muffled his hair. "You're a good boy, right, my brother?"

Peter was too embarrassed to look into his son's eyes. "Just lead us to your mother and the others." The harsh tone that remained in Peter's voice emotionally crushed the boy.

Andrew reluctantly left his nephew in his father's care in order to help Thaddaeus with Philip; he was no longer able to travel on his own. "Lead the way, Peter."

Still unable to look down into his boy's eyes, Peter pressed the flat of his hand against the youth's back and gave him a gentle push. "Go on, son. Lead us to safety."

CHAPTER 2

The Women

Philip fainted as soon as the front door was opened.

"My God." A woman peered into the early morning light from within the darkened threshold. "Get him in here before somebody sees this. Hurry."

Thaddaeus and Andrew held Philip upright between them and carried him inside with his feet dragging on the ground. As soon as Peter shut the door behind them, they hesitated at the relative darkness of the lamp-lit interior. It was too dangerous to leave the door open for daylight to enter or allow the charcoal remains that smoldered in a hole in the dirt floor to escape. Fortunately, the inhabitants were able to leave open the door leading to the roof to allow the pungent odor to escape rather than depending on the smoke to find its own way out through the cracks and crevices in the structure.

The women directed the men toward a corner on the second level of the tiny abode. This level, constructed of limestone, required two steps to mount, which Philip found difficult to climb without assistance.

"What happened to him?" the woman asked, as she embraced Eli, momentarily, relieved that he was safely with her once again.

Peter avoided answering her by directing his hard, guilty eyes upon his boy to prevent him from speaking as well. Philip didn't hear her, Thaddaeus ignored her, and Andrew stuttered and muttered and gave her the impression that the story behind Philip's injury was too complex to reveal to her at the moment.

"Mara, please," Andrew finally cajoled. "Take care of Philip first."

Mara studied Peter. "My husband seems particularly silent. It's not in character."

"We've been through a lot," Andrew implored.

"Right." Mara clapped her hands twice with a sharp precision that demanded everybody's attention. "Naomi, pour some water. Hanna, find a dry tunic. Miriam, feed the men." She continued to scrutinize Peter. "The rest of you, out of the way. Eli, Ira—accompany Leah to the roof and behave."

She waited for the young girl and two boys to respond before she addressed the somber men. "I don't like this, I—" she noted the growing irritation from her husband and quickly shifted her attention to Philip's medical needs. She climbed the two stairs and hurried to the injured man, who was already occupying a clean straw pallet. He was lying on his right side because of the wound and his knees were drawn toward his abdomen because of the pain. Mara kneeled beside him and touched his forehead. "He's burning up. Naomi, I'll need several linen compresses with that bowl of water."

"Coming."

Mara raised Philip's tunic above his waist to expose the bandaged sight. His loincloth was filthy and wet; his bandage and dressing were only marginally better. She leaned closely to him and whispered, "Everything needs to come off."

Philip responded with a wan smile, followed by a feeble nod of consent.

Mara located the bandage's knot under his right side, which held the dressing in place, and pried it loose.

Philip flinched.

"Sorry, dear." The bandage was easily unwrapped, but the dressing was stuck to the wound. Mara lifted a corner of the dressing to the point before it would begin to tear the clot. "Can't see a thing. Hanna, bring me a lamp."

Naomi set a large clay bowl, with several clean squares of linen floating in water, on the stone floor by Philip's pallet. "How does he look?"

"I'm not sure."

Hanna eagerly brought the small oil lamp and carefully directed the flickering light near Philip's wound.

"Thank you, dear," said Mara. Then she lifted one of the linen squares out of the water, gently wrung it out, and brought it near the wound. She lifted the corner of the dressing again and, this time, with the increased light, she was able to regard the redness and the swelling from the exposed edge of the injury. "Hmm. Not good. Maybe infected. Let's see." She wet the area underneath the lifted corner of the dressing to help loosen it from the clot.

Philip winced.

"Easy now. I'll try not to hurt you." She proceeded gently, but firmly, to pull the dirty dressing from the entry wound without causing heavy bleeding. To her surprise, she discovered that the dressing was also stuck to a wound in back. "My God, what have we got here?"

"It went all the way through my side," Philip dimly muttered.

"What went through?" Mara inquired, as she suppressed the concern in her voice.

"A knife."

"Hmm. Then a clean cut, perhaps. Let's find out. Take the light over to the other side of him."

Hanna laid the clean tunic she had also brought beside Mara before she maneuvered around the foot of the pallet; she wedged herself between Philip and the wall, where she could steadily shine the lamp's light on the side of Philip's lower back.

Mara shifted some of her concern toward Hanna. "I'm sorry. Are you alright?"

"Yes, yes, of course, Mara. I'm still two full months away from my first born." Hanna's large and dark brown eyes shined brightly from her youthful face, made more beautiful by her marble clear complexion and delicate features.

Mara nodded approvingly, then redirected her attention to Philip's injury. "Steady the light, dear." Mara also removed the other side of the dressing by continuously wetting underneath its lifted corner while gently pulling the cloth away from the soaked clot. "There. Red. Swollen. But clean, I think." She grabbed a fresh wet square of linen and washed the surrounding sight of both wounds.

Philip remained steady throughout the cleaning procedure.

"Whose knife?" Mara finally demanded.

Philip closed his eyes instead of answering her.

Naomi had prepared another large bowl of water and had set it at the foot of the pallet in order to wash Philip's feet and legs.

Together, the three women quietly cleansed Philip's multiple wounds, bathed him, and changed his tunic after removing his filthy loincloth. The procedure took several bowls of water, which Naomi provided by carrying each dirty bowl of water out through the side door into a small communal courtyard shared by several neighboring households, and dumping its contents into the mud. Then she'd replenish the bowl from one of several very large clay storage jars of water.

"Just hold the light steady," Mara instructed. "You've already had three miscarriages."

"I'm alright," Hanna said too optimistically. "I feel our Lord has blessed me this time. I'm alright."

"Nevertheless, don't do anything else. Just sit there with your back against the wall and hold the light."

Miriam listened carefully to the activities of the women, particularly to her mother, Naomi, as she tended to the needs of the men. She first provided them water to slake their thirst, then water for washing. Then she rolled out a small mat over the opposite corner, near the edge of the second level, to conduct an informal meal. She remained guarded by their morose dispositions and worked as invisibly as a woman, particularly a young woman of thirteen years, could become when serving men in silence.

Miriam quickly set out a bowl of parched corn and a bowl of pistachios, as well as separate bowls for raisins and dried figs. Yesterday's bread was all she could provide with a large chunk of white cheese and a small bowl of olives.

The men sat closely huddled around the mat and gazed sullenly at one another until Andrew took the initiative to offer thanks for the meal. "Blessed are you, Jehovah our God, King of the world, who causes to come forth bread from the earth."

Their disorienting gloominess persisted and kept them immobile, despite their intense hunger, for quite some time.

Thaddaeus yawned, then tore a piece of bread from a loaf. Andrew plucked an olive from its bowl and popped it into his mouth. Peter bit into a fig and began to chew.

They were too tired and preoccupied to taste their food. They dipped randomly into the bowls and ate whatever happened to be nearest their reach. They chewed their food slowly, grimly. Their blank stares kept Miriam feeling uneasy and cautiously attentive to the service of the meal. The only noise among them was the occasional crack of a pistachio.

Rather than replenish their cups with water, Miriam placed a flask of wine on the edge of the mat and awaited their response.

Peter grunted. "Wine."

Miriam quickly filled his empty cup with wine, knowing that it should have been milk, instead. But nobody had done the milking this morning; not after yesterday's horror, last night's weather, and this morning's surprise. Miriam became alarmed when she realized Andrew had been waiting with his raised empty cup for her to pour.

"Sorry," she whispered.

Andrew spoke gently to her as she nervously poured. "It's been a horrible night for all of us. Have the women been able to sleep?"

"Not for a single moment," Miriam said, as she went to Thaddaeus to pour wine into his awaiting cup.

Andrew studied Naomi's oldest daughter: Miriam was a strong, adolescent beauty nearly ready for marriage. She would bear healthy boys, no doubt, and keep a well-organized home. Her thick dark hair peeked out from the front edge of her loosely draped mantle, which framed her lovely face composed of delicate features similar to Hanna's. This drew Andrew's bachelor interest into further study: delicate features were not the norm and neither was his taste. Miriam's nose was narrow and pointed and its bridge rose and settled onto a narrow forehead. Her face was uncommonly smooth and uniform all the way to her neck—and beyond, Andrew imagined. He drank some wine and noted the fragility of her small mouth and wondered about its potential passion.

Andrew lowered his eyes and stared at the rim of his cup.

He still lived under Peter's roof with Mara and Eli, as well as with their widowed mother. Things would have to change for him, he thought. Living with Peter was no longer possible. But where would he go? What would he do? Would their Master really return from . . . from . . . from the dead, as he said he would? He wanted to believe this. He'd seen Jesus perform many wonders. And when with him, always when with him, everything seemed right. But now that he was gone— forever, perhaps—nothing felt right. Nothing seemed natural: his casual attraction for Miriam, his taste for food and wine, his relationship with Peter and the others, and his thoughts concerning spiritual matters in particular were stretched and distorted into something unrecognizable to him. In short, he'd lost himself; he'd lost his beliefs, his spirit, his understanding, his . . . his self. That's where it seems to begin and end, he thought. He shifted his eyes away from his cup and caught Thaddaeus studying him. Andrew flattened his animated expression back into the blank stare that they had been sharing.

Thaddaeus turned away from Andrew's piercing eyes, knowing that he would not suffer any resentment over the slight breach of privacy. He thought very highly of Andrew. In fact, other than their Master, he loved Andrew the most. He was a steady and dependable friend; honest to the bone and kind to his wife and two boys—even his young daughter. Living with someone on the road for years reveals everything and, therefore, he trusted Andrew with his life. He crammed a dried fig into his nervous mouth and began to chew; its dryness forced him to sip some of the wine Miriam had poured for him. Her female attentiveness suddenly raised his concern over the whereabouts of his wife. "Do you know what's become of my family?"

Miriam was startled by his address. "I . . . I believe they're safe. Mother . . . Mother, I believe, knows of their exact location."

"They're safe," Naomi confirmed reassuringly as she continued to assist Mara with Philip's medical needs. "A want-to-be Jerusalem disciple and his family have taken them into their home until . . . until . . ."

The long silence that followed intensified everybody's general concern and doubt and uncertainty.

"And, *my* mother?" Andrew inquired.

"She insisted on remaining at her side," Mara interjected.

"Whose?"

"Mary's. *His* mother."

"Ah. Yes." Andrew shot a furtive glance at Peter. "And, I suspect, alongside our Mary of Magdala, as well."

Mara wrinkled her brow to emphasize her conster-
nation. "But of course!" She dismissed Andrew and his
ridiculous inquiry by returning her full attention to
Philip's care.

Andrew successfully avoided Peter's pressing gaze
by reaching for a pistachio and attentively cracking it
between his teeth. But Thaddaeus was caught and held,
momentarily, by the panic in Andrew's brother's eyes.
He wrenched himself away from Peter's boiling gaze to
separate himself from its caged violence.

Peter was hurt by Andrew's avoidance and Thaddaeus's outright rebuff. He felt hopelessly alone and
helplessly trapped. There was nowhere for him to go:
nothing he could say to prevent the cause of Philip's
injury from being told; nothing he could do to turn
back the wheel of time in order to place him at his Master's side throughout the period that led him to the
agony of crucifixion. There was nobody he could turn
to: he was alienated from his fellow disciples despite
their open and sincere forgiveness and tolerance
toward him, alienated from his son, and soon to be
alienated from his wife.

Peter stirred uneasily and took a deep drink from
his cup as he thought: what about his own mother?
Would she also turn away from him once she discovered how despicably he'd acted in the last day or two?
All would be revealed, he thought with great agony. His
possessiveness of Jesus, his elbowing toward leader-
ship, his demands for attention and power and privi-
leged status among them had vanished in just a few
short hours. What happened? How could his Master

have allowed this to happen to him? Jesus must have seen through him all along. Jesus must have known how destructive the outcome was going to be. Jesus must have had a purpose for allowing this, for setting him up, for leaving him in this wretched circumstance!

Peter gulped down the rest of his wine and raised his cup for more.

Miriam filled his cup to the brim, sensing and fearing his mood. She glanced at Andrew and accidentally made eye contact.

Andrew was kind enough to keep her invisible by not addressing her. He shifted his attention to his brother. "You haven't eaten much, Peter."

"I need the wine more," Peter grumbled.

"Its effect won't do you any good," Andrew whispered sympathetically. He shifted his gaze to Miriam and emphatically jerked his tilted head in her mother's direction.

Miriam set the wine flask down on the edge of the mat near Peter, scanned the meal setting to make sure there was plenty to eat, then left them to conduct the remaining portion of this informal repast on their own. She made a valiant attempt to unobtrusively join the other women in Philip's attendance.

"What are you doing here?" Mara demanded.

Andrew anticipated his sister-in-law's reproach. "She's fully seen to our needs, Mara."

"But she's supposed to—"

"And, she's been dismissed."

Mara understood the inverted but carefully delivered reproof. She directed her seething response at Hanna. "Hold the lamp steady, will you?"

With Philip bathed, his loincloth removed, and his dressing changed and secured with another bandage, Mara shifted to the head of the pallet to help Philip sit up while Naomi unfolded the clean tunic.

"Raise your arm, dear," Naomi directed.

With difficulty, Philip responded to her instruction, which allowed her to loop the wide armholes through his uplifted arms and pull the tunic over his head so its open collar could drop around his neck. With Mara's assistance, Naomi wrestled with the tunic to get it past his chest and back, under his buttocks, and over his knees. Then as the older women helped Philip reposition himself comfortably on his back, Miriam took away the remaining bowls of dirty water while Hanna replaced the oil lamp into a nearby recess in the wall.

When Miriam returned from the courtyard with the empty bowls, she saw Hanna stretching painfully with the flat of her hands pressed against her lower back.

Hanna detected Miriam's concern and reassured the adolescent that her discomfort was insignificant with a surreptitious shake of the head, punctuated by her covertly compressed lips.

"He was a magician," Peter muttered almost inaudibly.

Thaddaeus was able to read his lips. "Of what importance is that now?"

Peter gazed at the small bowl of olives while Andrew and Thaddaeus waited breathlessly for another outrageous and discordant outburst.

"An illegitimate son of a Galilean peasant woman,"

Peter said tonelessly, "who made vagrants of tax collectors and sailors of the worst sort."

"Don't include me in that lot," his brother furtively countered.

Peter grunted ironically as he leaned closer to the other two men. "See? Hopeless. We're tattooed with his magic spells. *And*, we're deluded by *his* thinking that we are better men than we really are."

Andrew glanced at the women to see if they heard his brother's remark. "Think for yourself, Peter."

"One of us has to say the words."

"Those are not my words," Thaddaeus murmured.

"Why?" Andrew scorned. "And why you? Because you have failed miserably?" Andrew's face was twisted with disdain. "Don't blame magic."

"Why else would we have dropped everything and followed him at once," Peter persisted relentlessly. "I tell you, we were enchanted by a magician."

"Perhaps, you. Not me."

Peter was startled by the certainty in Andrew's voice. " '*Let the dead bury the dead*,' remember that?"

"He was demanding, yes."

"He was holy," Thaddaeus carefully interjected as he regarded the women's continued preoccupation with Philip.

"*And*, he required our complete obedience," Andrew said in support of Thaddaeus.

"But the Law—"

"Was to be followed, Peter, by those incapable of believing in him—"

"And his teachings."

"His life," Thaddaeus qualified, still trying to recover from the shock of Peter's persistently ugly remarks. "His teachings was his life."

"I believed in him," Peter said vacantly. He was breaking under the pressure of his brethren. "But I'm buried with questions. I'm drowning in questions."

"Then what are you saying?"

"Nothing." Peter buried his face in his hands.

Despite their best efforts, the women had begun listening to their heated discourse.

"His many cures were certainly not magician's work," Thaddaeus said with finality.

"And I'm convinced that his ability to command spirits and send them out of the possessed was also no slight of hand," said Andrew. Then he shook his head, bewildered by his brother. "How can you, Peter?"

"What?"

"You who walked on water. How can you still doubt him?"

Peter lowered his hands from his face. "It's self-doubt."

"Two sides of the same coin."

"Remember. I began to sink when—"

"If he could raise the dead, as we've seen him do with others," Thaddaeus proposed, "then why couldn't he raise himself like he said he would?"

"Ugh," Peter gasped. "More questions without possible answers."

"Time will give us the answers," Thaddaeus countered. "It must. It *must*."

"The time is now," Peter said morosely. "Now. But we are left empty and frightened and discarded."

The women listened with increased alarm. Doubt had not been a factor within them, even though fear and sorrow had shaken them to the core of their being.

"He forgave sins," Mara announced, breaching the gender wall of separation.

Hanna and Miriam held their breaths while Naomi's grim countenance was set and ready to support Mara.

"And by what authority do you speak?" Peter challenged.

"By . . . by none at all. These were our Master's powers." Her countenance competed with her husband's in the degree of sternness that could be projected. "How clever you are to doubt his words and actions now that he's no longer with us."

"I've always had *some* doubt."

"I did not see this *always* with you in his presence."

"Be careful, woman."

"Or what? These last many hours, which have separated us since yesterday, have been equal to a lifetime. You, me, *we* . . . are no longer what we once were anymore." She glanced at Naomi before addressing her husband. "We thought you'd been arrested with the others."

"What others?"

"Bartholomew and Paul and . . . and several others. They were arresting everybody last night and . . . and we assumed that . . . that—"

"You were arrested, as well," Naomi said, realizing that Mara was beginning to lose her confidence. She also recognized that Mara may have become understandably afraid to find out anything truly contrary about her husband. "So, since you weren't, what happened to you? Where were you and," she glanced at Andrew and Thaddaeus, "and you two, as well?"

The silence from the men was deafening. They glanced sheepishly at each other hoping for a volunteer to speak.

Naomi touched Mara's forearm to reassure her. "And what happened to Philip?"

"Just tend to his injury, Mara."

Peter's intimidating tone did not impress his wife this time. "You mean, injuries. What happened to his finger? The cut there is very deep."

"It's a bite," Andrew said.

"From what animal?"

"Human," said Thaddaeus.

Mara shuddered. "What kind of madness is this?"

"You don't want to know, my sister."

"Ohhh, but I do."

Once again, the men grew audibly silent.

Mara nervously licked her lips and sought Naomi's eyes for courage. "Look at all of you. I'm beginning to fear what I think I see." She focused her attention on her husband's torn tunic. "What happened? Where have you been? If not arrested, why didn't we see you at Golgotha? Why this silence? Who . . . who, bit, Philip?"

Peter looked acutely into Andrew's eyes. The tension between them was palpable. Andrew inhaled as if to speak, but Peter stood up and proclaimed his guilt before it could be revealed by someone other than himself.

"I bit Philip!"

Mara's voice wavered. "You?" She studied all the men and reassessed their battered condition. "And you, and—you did this to each other?"

Eli climbed halfway down the roof ladder and looked down into the room. "It's begun raining again. Ira and I wanted to . . . to . . . can we come inside?"

"Yes. Yes, of course," Naomi answered for his mother and father and uncle.

The added presence of the two boys and sweet little Leah diffused some of the intensity among the adults. The sound of the hard rain could be heard hitting the roof and a renewed sense of dampness returned with the multiple roof leaks that had developed due to the unusual amount of rain that had fallen ever since the death of their Master the day before.

Both boys, as well as the girl, were smart enough to remain silent among the arguing adults. They would have preferred to remain on the roof, but the heavy rain truly forced them indoors. They occupied themselves by rooting about the dwelling for available empty pots to place on the ground as receptacles for catching water that leaked through the roof. The dirt floor level of the interior was already muddy and the smoldering charcoal in the fire hole was smoking and hissing from the splatter of water.

"Eli, did you close the roof door?"

"Yes, Mother."

"And please put out what's left of that smoking charcoal."

"Yes, Mother."

94

Naomi sought the attention of her youngest daughter. "Leah, help Miriam clear the meal."

"Yes, Mother."

Both mothers directed their attention to Hanna, but Naomi allowed Mara to speak first. "We don't know how to thank you and your husband, Aaron, for offering us your home like this."

"We are truly beholden to you," said Naomi.

"My husband and I are more than happy to share what we have with you."

"I hope that will continue to be your wish."

"And why should there be any change in their hospitality?" Peter challenged.

Mara verbally lashed out at him. "You tell me!"

A flash of lightning, followed by a deep crack of thunder, separated the hostility between them.

Hanna was embarrassed. Naomi was supportive. Mara stood firm.

Eli lowered his eyes in shame. Ira looked away. Miriam and Leah sidled closer together for sibling support.

Andrew and Thaddaeus sat still and aloof and avoided looking up at Peter, who stood at the center of everybody's focus: his legs apart, his fists clenched, his eyes bulging with paranoia. His woman's challenge before the entire household increased his unbearable and partially hidden shame. He was about to bark viciously at Mara in response when Philip, who remained feverishly asleep, groaned piteously for attention.

The wind and the rain suddenly increased in ferocity, forcing water through every weakness in the roof and the walls. There was nothing that could be done about the wetness of the packed dirt floor, caused by the additional leaks.

Miriam was able to coax Leah and the two boys to help her mop up the stone floor on the second level with hand rags that were wrung into bowls and jars until they were full, then carried outside to be dumped. They were desperate for an activity to make them invisible from the adults, again.

"We should be at the end of the rainy season by now," Thaddaeus casually remarked.

The rain pounded the roof as the thunder rolled over them. Crevices in the structure flickered from the steady lightning.

"Is this the world coming to an end?" Andrew quipped.

"The end of one thing, perhaps, and the beginning of another," Mara prophesied.

"And what is the meaning behind that?" Peter demanded of his wife.

Mara directed her arid expression into the liquidity of his eyes, forcing Peter to avert his glare. "Where were you? Why didn't I see you at the foot of his cross?" The hollowness of her voice sent a chill up everybody's spine.

"Since when do you challenge me, woman?"

"Since . . . ever since we chose to follow Rabbi Jesus."

"That goes to show you how much you know. He chose us!" His bluster was sheer bluff and further eye contact with his wife was reduced to a series of short glimpses.

"Look at me, Peter. Look at me, I say!"

The entire household was shocked by her openly aggressive tone.

Andrew stood up. "Easy, Mara. Be careful. Think about what lines you are crossing over."

Lightning flashed and thunder cracked just as part of the eastside wall disintegrated and washed away from the lower level of the dwelling.

This series of events—the shouting, the thunder, the crumbling wall—startled Philip into semi-consciousness. "Peter, stop! Think about what you're doing! Stop!"

Hanna rushed to his side to calm him. She quickly removed the compress from Philip's hot forehead and freshened it in a nearby bowl of water. She wrung out the linen square, folded it, and placed the cool compress on his forehead. When she turned around to see what was happening, she discovered Mara standing over her with Miriam close by; the clustered men were inspecting the washed-away portion of the wall, while Naomi was herding Leah and the two boys to the opposite side of the dwelling.

"My husband has neglected his seasonal upkeep," Hanna confessed. "I warned him many times to repack these walls."

"It's alright," Thaddaeus said, in her husband's defense. "This happens even with the best mud brick."

"You don't have to make excuses for her husband," said Mara.

Thaddaeus shot his first hard glance at her. "Keep that tone directed toward your husband."

The steady reproach startled Mara into an involuntary cower, followed by a careful silence.

Andrew joined Thaddaeus to help diffuse the moment. "The mud from the lower wall has washed out into the narrow alley, Hanna. If we hurry, we won't have to level and repack the roof on that side. Does Aaron have a store of fresh brick?"

"Yes. Out there. Inside the attached shed in the courtyard." Hanna pointed to the west side for emphasis. "Through that side door."

"Good." Thaddaeus directed Peter and Andrew to join him.

The women could be heard talking as the men went outside into the courtyard:

"Aaron is such a procrastinator."

"You must learn to do it all, my dear."

"Men. They're not always dependable."

"Forget the always, Naomi."

Hanna and Miriam giggled nervously.

"Ira. Leah! Get away from that wall!"

The rain had eased up, the lightning had been reduced to a flicker, and the thunder could be heard in the distance.

The men congregated near the open entranceway of the shed, impervious to the outside wet conditions.

"It's awfully close in there," Andrew said.

"What are we going to tell them, for God's sake? What are—"

"Calm down, Thaddaeus."

"Ohhh, that's a good one. Peter telling me to calm down."

"Easy, both of you," Andrew said.

"These women." Peter ran his fingers through his hair. "They seem to make things more complicated than they are."

"No," Andrew countered. "It's not complicated. We abandoned him, clear and simple. Our explanation of this is what's complicated."

Thaddaeus shook his head. "I never thought I'd ever say this to you, Peter, but I feel sorry for you."

"For what?" Peter's response sounded like a bark.

"Well, I'm . . . I'm glad I don't have to face your wife."

"I'll handle her. Don't worry about that."

"Like you have this morning?"

"Stay out of this."

"Oh, believe me, I am. I just wish I were your brother. He doesn't have a wife to face, like you and I."

"Don't make it seem so easy and fortunate," Andrew balked. "I have someone just as serious to account to."

Thaddaeus smirked. "And who in this world would that be?"

"Myself."

The simplicity of Andrew's remark added tremendous weight to Thaddaeus and Peter.

"I believe you just doubled our mental burden," Thaddaeus said.

Andrew glanced at Peter. "Yes. Well. There's still some truth to your original statement, Thaddaeus."

"And that is?"

"I'm better off with myself than with Mara and myself."

"Enough of this, already," Peter grumbled. "We're beginning to sound like a bunch of women. We've got a wall to rebuild, remember?"

Peter and Thaddaeus squeezed into the shed and found a shovel, a mattock, a trowel, and a modest store of sun-dried mud bricks that were triple stacked to the height of the shed's back wall.

"There's plenty of dry brick in here to make a solid repair," Thaddaeus relayed to Andrew, who remained standing outside.

"Are there any tools?"

Thaddaeus handed the three implements to Andrew. "Start clearing the sight. Peter and I will haul the brick inside."

"Right." Andrew went to the side door leading into Aaron's dwelling, but paused momentarily before going inside. The rain had ceased.

Andrew was emotionally exhausted. He looked up into the overcast sky. Then he scanned the muddy courtyard, which would normally be full of domestic activity by the surrounding residents. Boys involved in heated competition, girls helping their mothers with the wash, elders sitting on a shaded bench had been wiped away by the odd weather.

He wondered if the tragic demise of his Master had had any influence on these absent inhabitants. His Master's name was not very well known and, yet, he'd seen his Master draw the multitudes. But in Jerusalem?—he wasn't sure. They hadn't been here long. Jesus' influence in the countryside had been great, but here . . . here in Jerusalem's rain, he wasn't so sure.

His Master's absence suddenly struck him and he became extremely lonely. What was he going to do now that he was empty of his presence? He was a follower, a student—and not a particularly bright one at that. Most of what Jesus taught him left him confused rather than enlightened.

He heard Thaddaeus and Peter stacking brick near the shed's opening. Andrew hurried inside to start clearing away the debris from the damaged wall.

Both boys and the girl had been sent up to the roof again with Miriam to get them out of the way. Hanna and Mara were still nursing Philip, and Naomi was standing by the wall inspecting its condition.

"Aaron's not very good with his hands," Naomi whispered.

"We can't be good at everything," said Andrew. "There are weaknesses in all of us."

"True. And there's certainly no weakness in his hospitality."

"Amen to that, sister."

"Can I help?"

"Yes," he whispered. "Try to keep Mara under control. At least until after this repair has been completed."

"I can only promise that I'll do my best," she mumbled.

Andrew laid the mattock and trowel on the floor, keeping the shovel in hand.

Naomi placed a gentle hand on his shoulder and

leaned close to him. She guarded the conspiratorial moment from Mara by keeping a careful eye on her as she lowered her voice to Andrew. "I will not judge. I swear. What's happened?"

"We . . . we, I—I acted cowardly and ran."

Naomi released a long breathy sigh. "And Peter?"

"Added denial to my . . . to his disgrace."

"It's no disgrace in avoiding crucifixion."

Andrew sucked in a short breath. "Thank you. You're the first . . . the first to speak to me with real sympathy and . . . and—" He leaned against the handle of the shovel. "I'm glad to receive any kind of consolation."

"It's not forgiveness," she cautioned. "I can't give you that."

"I know. But as you promised, it's not judgment, either." He searched her eyes for a clearer meaning. "I'll take whatever it was you meant."

"I don't know what I meant."

"Better yet. I don't know what I understood."

They heard Thaddaeus and Peter entering the side door.

"Quick! Go to Mara and, please, do what you can to keep her calm."

"I'll try."

Andrew got busy clearing the mud with his shovel while Naomi scurried to Mara's side.

The bricks were large and heavy and they were able to effectively carry only six at a time: three under one hand and three under the other pressed together in a short stack against their abdomens.

Peter called out to his brother. "How are you doing?"

"I'm still clearing out the mud."

Mara began to say something, but Naomi managed to still her with a cautioning gesture and a whispered plea to let them effect the wall's repair first, for Hanna's sake. Mara relented to the needs of her young hostess, realizing that the circumstances between her and her husband could wait. She kept silent, to Naomi's relief.

Andrew had caught the moment. He shut his eyes in a moment of thanks.

"Watch what you're doing," Peter growled. "You almost hit me with that damn shovel."

"Sorry. Glad the rain finally stopped."

"Yes, yes, whatever."

Andrew continued to clear the mud away while Peter and Thaddaeus went back to the shed to get more brick. Andrew stepped through the hole in the wall and shoveled the mud away from the outside wall. Then he reached inside, grabbed the trowel, and began squaring the opening to accommodate the new mud brick. By the time he was done, the other two had enough brick hauled to the sight to repair the wall.

"I'll lay the brick," said Thaddaeus.

"You any good?"

"I'm better than two fishermen."

"I've kept a healthy house all my life," Peter retorted.

"He was only kidding," Andrew interceded. "Calm yourself, will you?"

Peter bowed his head and sulked. "I can't seem to, damn it. I'm sorry, I'm sorry."

"Let's get this damn wall finished," said Thaddaeus, as he untwined the plumb line in order to hang it near the squared opening. "I take pride in erecting straight walls."

Andrew gave a sidelong look at Naomi who gestured that she was doing her best despite their constant bickering while mending the wall.

Hanna caught the exchange, but remained neutral.

The men worked more cooperatively for the next couple of hours.

Andrew relinquished the trowel to Thaddaeus, who laid the brick that Peter handed to him. Then Andrew provided Thaddaeus with constant buckets full of mud that was thick enough in consistency that it could be used for brick mortar.

Thaddaeus worked like an artisan, laying the brick level and plumb and thickly mortared enough so that cutting the fresh brick to fit the closing edges of the wall was kept to a minimum. He also managed the mortar so that the final top layer of bricks could be wedged into the remaining space between the top wall that had not fallen and the newly constructed one. If allowed to dry, it was reasonable to hope that the addition of the lower wall would be load-bearing enough to keep the upper wall in place.

Thaddaeus stood up from his kneeling position and stretched. Then he studied the wall. "This should hold. That is, if this damn rain has really come to an end."

Andrew nodded approvingly at the new wall before he revealed a sardonic smile.

"What?" said Thaddaeus.

"Rain."

"What about it?"

"It rhymes with pain."

"Don't be silly."

"And it came with our Master's death. Now that it has stopped, will he return?"

"You speak like a boy," Peter admonished.

"It wouldn't hurt you to show a little sentiment in your behavior," Mara challenged from across the room. Her temperament was similar to her husband's: hot and argumentative, dominant and combative. She'd held her tongue long enough.

Peter had gathered the tools and had them in his hands. He looked down and stared at them as if he was unaware as to how they came to be in his possession. He looked at Thaddaeus, then at Andrew, who lowered his eyes in sympathy.

"Well?" Mara shouted.

Peter imploded with internal rage, which made him tremble. He threw down the tools and directed his full attention toward her. "Well, what!"

"I've already asked too many questions without receiving any answers!"

"Upstairs, woman." He pointed to the roof. "Upstairs, now," Peter ordered. The strain in his voice had been filtered through his clenched teeth. The veins in his temples bulged with anger.

Mara was not impressed. She faced Peter with open defiance and made sure that he understood her lack of intimidation as she approached the interior ladder leading to the roof.

Everybody had grown quiet and had become unwilling to act as an intermediary between their growing domestic viciousness.

Mara grabbed the beam of the ladder, then scanned the interior room full of people. Eyes quickly averted, heads turned, small activities resumed. She remained in this position for an uncomfortably long period of time in direct defiance toward Peter. And just before Peter began to address her, she lifted her left foot onto the first rung of the wooden ladder. But, again, she purposely stalled her departure to increase Peter's fury.

"Woman," he seethed.

She slowly turned her head to him and revealed the smirk on her face. "Simon-Peter," she said sarcastically. "You should have remained Simon for all the loyalty you've shown to our Lord Rabbi."

Peter approached her menacingly. "Upstairs."

She started climbing. "Peter: the man of rock, indeed. You're not worthy enough to be a chipped fragment of a rock." She looked down at Peter with tremendous contempt before disappearing through the opening of the roof.

Peter glanced at Thaddaeus and Philip, then at his brother, with embarrassment. He chose visual contact with them in order to avoid the questioning eyes of the others in the room. He dashed to the ladder and quickly climbed it to the roof to escape the oppressive atmosphere.

She was waiting for him at the farthest corner of the roof; her left calf was braced against the parapet.

Eli, Ira, Leah, and Miriam were focusing steadily upon the game they had devised to preoccupy themselves. Like the adults below, they were trying to avoid getting involved in Mara's violent confrontation with her husband.

"Eli. Miriam. Go downstairs," Peter said flatly. "And take the other two with you." They did not respond quickly enough to his taste. "Now!"

They scurried to the roof's opening and assisted each other in hurriedly climbing down the ladder without uttering a word or showing a hint of protest.

Mara crossed her arms over her bosom to further express her contempt.

"Don't push me any further, woman. I'm warning you."

"Oh, how brave you are against women—and boys."

"Mara—"

"What? Are you going to strike me or stab me with a knife, as well?"

"Who told you about that?"

Mara was stunned, momentarily. "Then . . . then it's really true?"

"Bah, the truth."

Mara was dazed. "You bit his finger."

"So?"

"I didn't want to believe it was possible. But then I thought: if you bit his finger like that, you were capable of . . . of sticking, a knife, into, one of us."

"It was an accident."

"Your torn tunics and battered faces have told me otherwise. Don't add lying to your other grievous offenses."

"Who are you to judge me?"

"I don't know who you are. You could have killed Philip."

"It wasn't like that."

"Then tell me."

"I don't have to explain anything to you, woman." Peter smashed his right fist into his left palm for emphasis.

Mara was undaunted; her petulance increased. "Go on, act like a Greek—no—a Roman. Go on, strike me, Roman!"

"You . . . you wench." Peter stamped his heavy right foot on the flat roof. Water oozed over his sandals and between his toes from the saturated brushwood covering that lay across the heavy sycamore beams that supported them. He searched the empty roof for something to fix his gaze upon, but there was nothing. So, he walked to the opposite corner of the roof and posted himself under a crudely erected shade booth, which offered relief from the harsh-feeling light of the late morning sun that had temporarily broken through the overcast sky.

She pursued him aggressively. " '*I will make you fishers of men*,' " she mocked. "Go back to fishing creatures of the sea!"

Peter grabbed one of the four posts of the shade booth with his left hand to prevent himself from dashing toward her. "I walked on water. I walked on water to go to Jesus!"

"And you cried out like a boy when you sank, as the others have testified."

"You witch."

Mara pantomimed the act of drowning with her undulating arms above her head. "Lord! Lord save me!"

"Stop it!"

"How much proof do you need? What does it take to make you a man?"

Peter shook his huge right fist at her as he held onto the shade booth post. "I said—"

"Ah, yes," she said. "You always remember your strength. But you always forget that he was the Son of God."

"That's not true!"

"Then your actions betray you."

"I can't control that, Mara."

She shook her head with great judgment. "He has never been able to make anything of you. Go back to catching fish!"

Peter grabbed the post with both hands like a little boy. "I've tried, I've tried, oh God, I've tried not to see him as the Son of Man."

"You simple idiot. Trying to make you a leader among men is hopeless. Go back to being an ordinary Simon. You've never been the Peter he's wanted you to be. You're a disgrace. Go back to catching mackerel!"

The last series of remarks cut deeply into Peter's feelings. Bile and bitterness rose to the back of his throat and manifested itself into a scathing glint from the corners of his eyes. "I loved him. I loved him and . . . and, yet, I'm nothing. I followed him and . . . and, yet, I forsook him, I denied him, I failed him." Peter released the post and bowed his head in bitter shame.

"If you know so much, how come you're so stupid and loud and inattentive?"

Peter's lips trembled with loathing. "Shut up, woman. You don't understand anything." He ran his fingers through his hair, then self-consciously pulled and scratched at his beard. "I admit I'm hasty and hot-tempered. I admit I speak without thinking. I admit I wade into waters too deep for me. I admit, damn it. God, I admit. I'm . . . I'm so sorry."

"You're such an ungrateful boy," Mara said with enormous contempt. She stood before him filled with condemnation.

"Can I help it if I'm outspoken?"

"No," she said. "But you're usually wrong."

"I'm impulsive."

"You're mistaken."

"I have my doubts."

"You depended on him. You still do! What do you think he was all about? *'Believe in me,'* he said. *'Believe in me,'* not your pathetic, lost, self."

Peter smashed his right fist into the palm of his left hand. "I'll not be weak!"

"Then you'll not be strong!"

Peter stepped out from under the crude shade booth. "Don't you use his words against me."

"Your pride has always made him your adversary."

Peter raised his left hand to his brow to shade his squinting eyes. "How can you say that! I loved him!"

Mara grinned. "As you love me?"

His words were uttered very slowly and singularly. "You, are, evil, spirited."

"And you're a proud, self-centered braggart." Mara was relentless. She would not give him any leeway.

Peter was trapped in bad water. His soul was in peril. While avoiding a shoal, he was about to smash into rock. He turned away from his wife. "He loved me anyway." His back stiffened proudly in a sudden display of confidence. "No matter how ugly and repulsive I must appear to you, he loved me anyway!"

"Y–e–s." Mara softened. "That seems to be the shame of it. His forgiveness of you, of me, of all of us has cost him his life."

"Don't throw that into my face! Rome nailed him to the wood. How can you say otherwise?"

"I don't. I don't, really." Mara turned away from him for the first time and looked out along the rooftops of the city. "And yet, his sacrifice . . . there was . . . there was something of a sacrifice, which I felt, as I stood at the foot of his cross."

"Stop throwing your presence before him into my face!"

"That's right." Mara's eyes widened with disdain. "You slime. It always goes back to you. Yes. It's always about you and your prejudices."

"So? I'm reckless!"

"No. You're cautious."

Peter pranced about the roof like an injured

gamecock. "Was it cautious of me to draw a sword when they came to arrest him?"

"You knew he'd stop you."

"I cut off an ear!"

"And he healed it. You knew that would be so. You knew you'd be safe in that kind of act."

"You bitch. You slut."

"That's right. Go back to your old fisherman's habit of swearing."

He pointed an impotent finger at her. "I will. I'll . . . I'll do as I like, woman!"

"Yes. That has always confirmed your degradation."

He lowered his accusing finger. "But . . . but you misjudge me when my heart rules my head!"

"Heart, is it?" Mara cackled. "My, my, you certainly can justify yourself."

"I'm allowed. I was nearly his equal."

"Ohhh, and how you value your own importance." She pranced toward him to physically display her derision, then she planted herself firmly before him. "You presumptuous fool. Rebuke me, but not him; correct me, but not him; compare yourself to—and, yet, you dared. At times, you actually thought you knew better than our Master."

Peter felt the nakedness of his disgrace. "I . . . I couldn't help myself."

"You were tempted."

"I relied on myself," he said proudly.

"And I stood at the foot of his cross," she said. "Where were you? I didn't care about my own life. Where were you?"

"Leave me alone."

"I stood at the foot of his cross without you, Peter."

"Yes."

"Where—"

"Yes!"

"There's nothing wrong with being afraid, my dear."

"Yes," Peter said as he shuddered with grief. "But I was more than afraid. I was a coward."

"And?"

"He might have forgiven me, but I . . . I haven't forgiven myself."

"Grow up, Peter. This . . . this is not only about you."

"But who was he, really? I'm still not clear—not clear about him at all. Was he a magician, like they say? What? What kind of prophet was he?"

"You doubted Jesus all along," she said sternly. "Questioned him. Misunderstood him. Resisted him. In all that lies your present madness. I can't help you there. I can't make you think clearly."

"Yes, yes, I admit, I'm not a smart man. I'm a follower. But he . . . he placed me in the position of being a leader. And this has been a great burden to me."

"Don't hand me that! You placed yourself."

"I relied on myself, I told you!"

"Where were you!"

Peter winced at the impending doom of his inevitable verbal admission. "You know already."

"Let's hear it," she pressed relentlessly. "I want to hear it from my own husband's mouth. Why? Why was

I without you at the foot of his cross?" Her voice rasped with intensity. "Why."

"Because. Because I was in hiding. Because I ran. Because I was frightened!"

"And that's what you meant when you said, 'more than afraid.' "

"Yes."

"This has nothing to do with growing up."

"I was a coward, plain and simple."

"This has to do with the safety of the other disciples." She studied Peter as if he were an unfamiliar person. "I've always known you were selfish and mean-spirited, but I could never have imagined—"

"Stop it. If you know what's good for you, you'll stop this imagining."

"You spiritual dwarf," she sneered. "Ohhh, but you got what you wanted. Upon *you* he was to build—" she laughed. "What a leader you are, hiding and groveling in back streets like a frightened dog."

"Alright, I have my faults!" Peter countered defensively. "Woman, leave me be!"

Eli poked his head through the roof's opening. A concerned expression illuminated his face.

"What are you doing up here?"

"I was concerned for Mother and—"

"Me, I hope!"

The boy was petrified. "Yes. Yes, Father."

"Sure you were," Peter said sarcastically. "Get below before you feel the back of my hand across your face."

Eli snatched a glance at his mother, who encouraged him with a furtive nod to obey his father. Despite his apprehension, he managed to convey a formidable glare at his father as he lowered himself down the ladder and out of their presence.

"Hurt one hair on that boy and I'll—"

"What. What will you do, woman?" He shook his head with disbelief. "What kind of a man do you think I am? I have faults!"

"Then turn away. *'Get behind me, Satan!'* " Mara allowed her upper mantle to fall to her shoulders.

"I'll take that from Jesus, but not from you!"

"You'll take what I dish out, or you can leave!"

"Even Jesus didn't berate me as harshly as you!"

"That's because you performed well in front of him. Whenever you were able, you always said what he wanted to hear."

Peter felt the heat of shame throughout his body. "First you say I questioned him, now you say I supported him."

"Like the wind." Mara pulled her mantle off her shoulders and waved it about like a veil. She danced like a pagan Greek. "Like the changing wind." She pulled the mantle from the air as quickly as she had set it afloat and let one end of it drop to the roof's surface. " *'And whom do you say I am, Peter?'* " she mimicked. " *'You are the Christ, the Son of the living God.'* " She sneered at him. "Christ, you said. In Greek, even. My, how you squirmed for the position of power among all the disciples. My, how you could kiss his feet when the notion overtook you."

"I have my moments," he justified.

"You have defects, you mean."

Peter physically slumped from the sudden intensity of mental depression. "He loved me."

"And you repaid him with scandalous conduct."

He approached her. "You coldhearted hag."

Mara stood her ground. "The truth is without temperature. The truth simply is."

"The truth! The truth. What is truth?" Peter began to weep. "I denied him. I denied him completely—three times. Then . . . then the cock crowed, like he said." He was drunk with internal pain. "He predicted my loss of faith."

"He predicted your cowardice, if you ask me."

Bitter tears began rolling down Peter's cheek. He shuddered with rage: "I walked on water." He whispered: "I defended him with a sword." He sobbed: "I'm fearless, I tell you."

"You are soft with contradiction. In fact, you're no better than Judas in that."

Peter was stupefied. "Judas. Why Judas?"

"Because, sometimes, you think like a gentile."

"Damn it, woman, quit tormenting me!"

"I've only begun, you faithless wonder. You spiritless monster. You knife-wielding criminal. You dog-biting—"

Peter grabbed her by the throat, but did not cut off her breathing. "He said he would give me the keys to the Kingdom of Heaven."

Instead of being sensible, Mara became more belligerent and verbally abusive. "Then where are they? See? As you've admitted, he knew you'd deny him—

and you did, you pitiful piece of dung. You denied him more than once even. You coward," she spat venomously. "You low-crawling creature in the dust of—"

Peter cut off her air by choking her in earnest.

Mara's bulging eyes reflected the panic of her realization: she had crossed the line. With her hands hooked desperately on his forearms, she struggled helplessly to pull his powerful hands from her throat. But he was killing her in earnest. The blankness in Peter's eyes revealed a complete lack of reason.

Both of them struggled near the edge of the parapet: one for life, the other for death.

Mara released his powerful forearms and began hitting him with her fist wherever she could. She struck his face, his shoulders, his side, his leg, and then in a final moment of desperation she jerked her right knee into his groin as hard as she could. He released her after she delivered another blow to his groin.

They turned away from each other, broken people. Mara caressed her throat and gasped for air; Peter held his groin and gasped in pain. They stumbled about the roof like a couple of lost spirits searching for a way to escape eternity.

Mara managed to reach the shade booth to take advantage of its cover. She sat heavily on the adjacent parapet, which ran along one side of the booth near that edge of the roof. She took a deep breath. She cleared her throat. "If I hadn't really loved you, do you think I would have allowed you to abandon our life for this Jesus? Do you think I would have been here now?" She inhaled deeply, then exhaled slowly into a sigh.

"But now, now that I've learned to love him, now—*now* where are you? *Now*, where were you in his hour of need? Where . . . who . . . who are you, now?"

Peter released his groin and cautiously approached her. "I . . . I don't know. I don't know. I'm sorry. Forgive me, please. Please, forgive me."

She placed her right hand against her face. "I'm hot." She ignored him.

Peter shivered. He leaned against one of the shade booth's posts. "This is madness. Cruel forgiveness. I can't take it!" He struggled and squirmed internally, like a madman, as he slid down the post and sat on the soggy rooftop. The shock of the cool wetness seeping into his tunic and loincloth startled him, but he was too filled with exhaustion to rise from the rooftop's muck. He stroked his beard, instead.

Mara cleared her throat, again. "This has been a horrible two days for both of us. It's been, well—a great loss. A great loss." She massaged her throat. "I almost deserved this. I . . . I should have used better judgment." Peter started to say something, but she gestured, with the flick of her left hand, for him to keep silent. "But this moment ends what was left between us. No. Don't say anything, please. It's been coming for quite some time: what with living on the road, hand to mouth, and always uncertain about the future, always confused about his teachings. It's been too much. Too crazy. Too emotional. And between *his* and *your* constant scrutiny, well, there were times I was so afraid to offend either one of you that . . . that I couldn't see straight. I was dropping things and burning food and stumbling over my words for no reason. I was a mess, a mess, until—until that one day, that day when our Master stopped me from my frantic activity and said: 'Unnecessary. All unnecessary. Relax. It's already done. There are no gains or losses. Nothing and everything matters.' "

She straightened her back. "I suddenly realized that his expectations of me were my own, self-imposed, expectations. I wasn't in between anybody, I . . . I was simply opposite you. You. And when he saw me catch this . . . this glimpse of you, who was finally standing at a distance from me, he said: 'Someday he'll realize— he'll understand this kind of unnecessary.' " She lifted and held her head high. "I was suddenly awakened . . . awakened from a strange dream. And when I took another glimpse of this you that was no longer me, I saw someone who was still living in a dream. I saw a you without me caught in the illusion of struggle. It was a you who believed he was somewhere leading us to else-where." She deflated, slightly, with an exhale. "From that moment on, I no longer loved you as my husband. I loved you as a fellow man who needed love more than he could give it because . . . because he did not under-stand that it was already done. Already done."

Peter stirred restlessly. "I . . . I don't understand."

"And I can't help you." Mara stood up to empha-size her dismissal of him. "I'm leaving you, Peter."

He stood up, as well, to meet her unflinching gaze. "But . . . but you can't."

"It's a new day, Peter. And I have nothing more to lose."

"But Eli—"

"Is almost a man, who will watch out for my practical interests, as necessary."

"You're a woman—"

"Of Palestine. Precisely. And he's my devoted son, who will accompany me as I continue to follow our Master's teachings."

"But you . . . you can't leave me."

"In my mind, I already have."

Peter looked out along the multitude of empty rooftops. There was a strange, deserted feeling at this level of the city. Its geometrical whitewashed face, dotted with crude shade booths, created an eerie landscape akin to a desert's monochromatic wilderness. He was lost within this unfamiliar geography. Lost and desperate and impotent. "You . . . you can't leave me. Don't you remember? You were there when our Master prohibited such actions from . . . from either of us."

"Yes, and he often went too far."

"You question his words, now? Why not when he was with us?"

"No," she said peevishly. "I question my understanding of his words. Always."

Peter shook his head. "He pleased nobody with his views on divorce. Shocking. It was simply shocking."

"To you, perhaps. But for me, and other women, his views were an improvement."

"I've never treated you badly," Peter countered fretfully.

Mara grimaced. "Typical. Every time our Master made us more equal, I heard your resentment."

"Well, he . . . he often went too far!"

"You question his words now? Why not when he was with us?"

Peter's face turned crimson with rage. "Don't get smart with me. Don't you use his . . . my words, against me!"

"They were mine, first! And I'll do what I please. I have as much, if not more, understanding of his teachings as you do."

"That still doesn't make you equal to me, woman."

"According to our Master, once married, we are joined together by God forever. That makes us more equal."

"Then you can't divorce me," Peter said, patently pleased by his conclusion.

"Who says I'm divorcing you?"

"But—"

"I'm leaving you. As someone more equal."

"Bah! A loophole."

"His words! My words, now."

"And what will you do?" Peter sneered.

"Speak on this message."

"No one will listen."

"That's right. There are plenty of no ones who bear newborns."

"Ugh, women."

Mara's eyes glazed over with introspection. "Our Master was a true revolutionary. To think, he included me, a woman—in fact, all women—when he said, *'The days are coming when people will say, how lucky are the women who never had newborns, who never bore babies, who never nursed them.'*"

"Bah! I never heard him say that!"

"That's because you were in hiding like a frightened rat!"

"Watch it."

"That's because he spoke to those women, me among them, who managed to get through the crowd and stay close to him—especially, when he fell."

"Fell?"

"Yes. One of several times on his way to Golgotha!" She took a deep breath. "He heard us weeping for him. Us! And he tore himself away from his pain long enough to speak to us of this freedom."

"Nonsense."

"Yes. Nonsense." Mara spoke as if in a distant vision. "In his fall, therein lies our rise to freedom."

"That's a lunatic's interpretation. A visionary fiction."

Viciously. "You weren't there. You'll never know any other meaning!"

"Absurd."

"No less absurd when he told us to reject our mothers and brothers in favor of the family of his followers. Remember that?"

Peter's eyes darted from side to side with confusion. "Yes. *Yes*. Yes! Who could understand his every word?"

"Right. Even his mother couldn't. Poor dear. She didn't get to hear her son's most liberating words while on his way to Golgotha because of the crowds."

"*Liberating*. Liberating according to you."

"And who else? It's always . . . always according to this . . . this *you*."

The sudden pounding of the main door below alarmed them. Mara peered over the parapet to the street below and discovered a squadron of legionnaires. "Romans!"

"What?"

Peter leaned over the parapet beside her to see for himself.

The pounding grew louder. "Open this door! In the name of Caesar, I command you to open up!"

Mara was shocked by their numbers. There was a sea of helmets and shields, lances and swords of destruction at their door. "Look at their number."

Peter had been counting. "Between thirty and forty of them. Over three squads with a centurion, no less. With a centurion. We are not important enough for this heavy a show of force."

One of the soldiers below caught sight of them. "Up there! Look out!"

Peter pulled Mara and himself away from the parapet. "I don't understand. We're simply not that important!"

Eli poked his head through the roof's opening. "Mother! Romans!"

"We can see that, boy!" Peter hissed. He rushed to the roof's entrance. "Out of my way."

The boy scurried down the ladder as his father stepped onto a top rung to lower himself inside. As soon as his head cleared the rooftop, he heard the front door being pulled open. He discovered that his brother had had enough presence of mind to respond to the legionnaire's command. By the time Peter was halfway down the ladder, the soldiers had poured into the tiny abode.

"Everybody stay where you are!" The centurion observed Peter on the ladder and pointed his drawn sword at him. "Stop right there!"

The poverty of the dwelling's inhabitants was accentuated by the polish of the enemy's armor and the lively colors of their garments.

The women and their young were huddled near Philip at the corner of the dwelling. Andrew was standing by the opened doorway with the point of a sword pressed perilously against his vulnerable throat and Thaddaeus was standing near the side door, looking as if he'd been caught trying to escape into the courtyard.

"You. Come down from that ladder," the centurion ordered.

Peter stepped down carefully. He glanced up at the roof's opening, hoping Mara would remain silent.

"Is there anybody else left on the roof?"

"No," said Peter.

Mara stepped on the top rungs of the ladder and began climbing down.

"Liar," said the centurion.

"He's not a liar!" Mara countered. "Since when is a woman anybody?"

Mara's mean-spiritedness amused the centurion and several of the legionnaires. "Then he's not a liar, according to you."

"He's a coward, among other things, but not generally a liar."

The soldiers laughed resoundingly.

With increased humor, the centurion addressed his men. "Not generally, she says." Their laughter intensified. "Which one of you is the husband of this shrew?"

"I am," Peter said.

"Ah, yes, of course. Anyone else on the roof?"

"No."

The centurion stepped toward Peter. "You don't look to be a coward by the size of you." The centurion gestured to a couple of soldiers to go topside and search the roof. They jovially climbed the ladder and disappeared through the roof's opening. "Your wife could be heard shrieking all the way to the lower part of the city."

"I can't control what my wife does."

"Obviously. But you need to. Because that's why I'm here. Not that any of you are of the least importance to me."

"Then why are there so many of you? I counted nearly four squads outside."

"That's none of your concern. But now that we're here," he glanced at one of his senior men, "have the men conduct a complete search of the area, including the courtyard."

The soldier saluted him. "Yes, sir."

"In fact, search inside the nearby dwellings for weapons, as well. Arrest anybody suspicious. Anybody."

"Yes, sir." The senior man directed several legionnaires to inspect the interior of Aaron's dwelling before he went outside to direct the remaining squads to search the entire surrounding district.

They watched helplessly as the destructive legionnaires turned the interior of Aaron's dwelling upside down, breaking and smashing anything that was fragile enough to destroy without effort.

"There's no need for your men to tear this home apart," Mara challenged.

"Don't make me regret my careless tolerance, woman," the centurion firmly cautioned.

"But, but why so many of you?" Peter carefully inquired. "We're . . . we're nobody."

"That's right." The centurion was amused by Peter and his outspoken wife. "And, as I said, your nobody shrew is what drew you to our attention as we were marching by toward the lower end of the city. There have been numerous groups of bandits prowling the night streets looting and destroying and inciting the general populace into near riots in some sections of the city. I've been told that their leaders are the remnants of one of those who was crucified yesterday. The one Pilate called, your King." The centurion noticed the general spread of discomfort among the inhabitants.

One of the soldiers involved in the interior's search pushed Naomi and Leah aside to reach Philip. "There seems to be an injured man over here, sir."

The centurion's eyes brightened. "Ahh, what luck." The centurion climbed the two steps onto the second level and approached Philip. "Who is this? What's wrong with him?"

"The man is sick," said Mara.

"I see." The centurion scanned the silent men. "Does she usually speak for the men of this house?"

"I can speak," Philip said weakly. He tried unsuccessfully to sit up. "I have a fever."

"I recognize the bulge of a dressing under a tunic when I see one."

"I don't deny the injury. I . . . I fell accidentally, fell onto the point of a trowel that pierced my side."

"That's right," Peter inserted. "We were repairing a washed-away wall."

Thaddaeus weaved warily around several legionnaires as he crossed the length of the second level. He stepped down to the lower room, approached the sight of the repaired wall, and indicated the nearby tools to support Peter's statement. He even picked up the plumb line, separated the stone anchor that was tied to the end of the ball of line, and began to untwine the rig in order to demonstrate something of his actual abilities.

The centurion approached Thaddaeus, not fully convinced. "Drop it." Thaddaeus lowered the plumb line to waist level and cocked his head to one side to reveal his confusion. "I said drop it!"

Thaddaeus dropped the stone plumb line as if he suddenly realized he'd been handling a poisonous serpent.

"Certainly, you don't think he'd use that as a weapon against you," Andrew said, who was still standing near the doorway with the point of a legionnaire's sword pressed against his throat.

The centurion turned to Andrew and gestured at the legionnaire to lower his short sword. "And who are you?"

Andrew jutted his chin toward Peter. "His brother."

"Ahh. And, therefore, this shrew's brother-in-law."
The centurion grinned to encourage his men to laugh.

"We've done nothing to incur Caesar's wrath. Domestic. Purely domestic is our trouble."

The centurion resheathed his sword into his scabbard. "Not unless I—your Caesar at this moment—say so." He noticed the trowel and picked it up. "So, is this the implement that caused the injury?"

"It is," said Thaddaeus.

"Hmm. I don't see any evidence of blood."

"It was washed off, of course."

"Of course."

The centurion climbed up to the second level and approached Philip with the trowel. "Is this what caused your injury?"

Philip nodded, yes. He was sweating profusely with fever and he was pale with fatigue. Philip tried to focus his attention on the centurion's stern countenance, but he was near the edge of unconsciousness once again.

"Let's see his wound."

"For the love of God," Peter said.

The centurion turned to Peter with extreme displeasure and brandished the trowel at him. "I don't have any love for your God. Do you understand that? God." He spat on the ground. "Gods. A foolish business, all of it." He pointed to the opened front door. "My standard bearer waiting outside holds the spirit of the Roman Empire: the eagle of my legion, the image of my Emperor. That's what I revere, that's my only allegiance, that's my reality. Rome. Caesar: the ruler of

the world. That's certainly not anything imaginary like
. . . like a god. Particularly your empty and invisible
god."

"All's clear on the rooftops, sir!"

"Very well!"

"All's clear in the courtyard, sir!"

"Very well!"

The centurion studied the trowel for a long period
of time, twirling it very slowly by its wooden handle.
He examined the implement with so much intensity
that it appeared as if he fully expected the crude object
to reveal its truth to him. He tore his eyes away from
the trowel and leered at Philip. "The wound. Let's see
it."

Naomi went to Philip's side. "He's too sick to show
you without my assistance."

"Are you his wife?"

She hesitated. "Yes."

The centurion pursed his lips in a display of cyni-
cism. "Another lie."

The senior legionnaire reentered the dwelling
through the side door. "All seems to be in order, sir. All
is secure."

"And everyone denies any wrongdoing, correct?"

"Of course, sir," said the senior men. "This is Palestine."

"And it's a verifiable fact that everything and everybody in Palestine smells of a lie to us," the centurion
added.

"Yes, sir."

The centurion lowered his hard gaze at Naomi,

who was kneeling beside Philip. "Well? I haven't got all day."

"She'll need my help," Mara said.

"Then help her, damn it!"

Mara rushed over to Philip to assist Naomi. She got behind him and helped him to sit up, while Naomi reached for a dry towel in order to cover Philip's genitals before raising the lower end of his tunic above the dressing.

"Hurry up, I said." The centurion was growing bored. "I'll not urge you again."

Naomi untied the bandage and carefully removed the dressing.

The centurion stepped closer to Philip. "Shine a lamp."

Naomi grabbed the nearby lamp from the wall's recess and brought its feeble flicker near Philip's wound.

The centurion studied the wound for a very long time.

Peter glanced at Andrew. Thaddaeus held Philip's unsteady gaze.

Naomi sought Mara's hard eyes, while Miriam and Ira made sure their younger siblings stood firmly uncommitted.

The legionnaires receded into their usual and familiar torpor state, a condition that was the direct result of having to wait through long periods of empty time until their superior was ready to issue his next order to them.

The centurion seemed mesmerized by Philip's

injury, as well as lost in his own presence. He was richly dressed with an expensive red woolen tunic under a light suit of chest armor that was partially covered in back by a thick water-resistant robe. His helmet was the only headgear among these four squads of legionnaires to bear the colored plume of his unit. And because of his relatively superior wealth, the scabbards of both his long and short shorts were ornately decorated with the images of various pagan gods.

He was an extremely stern-looking, Roman-born man in his prime: a tough professional soldier who could demonstrate as much brutality as necessary without being excessively cruel. He was a rational day-to-day officer in the regular army who was able to train, supervise, and lead his predominantly Syrian auxiliary Palestine forces to do whatever he was commanded to do.

Based on his general behavior, the centurion seemed to be almost reasonable and especially cautious in character. He could have simply arrested them all and destroyed the dwelling without thought. No one would have questioned him, certainly not his superiors. But then, what was he doing? What was he looking at? What was he thinking?

The Syrian legionnaires were a different class of being. They were a rough and rugged illiterate bunch who were used to boring guard duty, daily training, heavy physical labor, poor food, and sour wine; they were also ready for the possibility of death in battle. This highly trained foot soldier did not usually care about the prevailing political atmosphere or how he was perceived by the local population. They were relatively well-equipped, disciplined soldiers who were trained to fight bandits or whole armies or to, simply, lead prisoners to their places of execution.

These auxiliaries also carried a long and a short sword, as well as a simple javelin that served as a lighter pilum and a large convex oval shield. Their chest armor was cruder and lighter than the centurion's and their helmets were unadorned. Their service-issued tunics were made with a coarse wool that was dyed with a lusterless red, a hue created by the addition of cheap brown coloring in the dying mixture. They were equipped like any usual auxiliary legionnaire: lighter and inferior to that of the regular army.

"Are you going to stand there all day?" Mara taunted. "Or are you going to tell us why his injury is so important to you?"

The centurion burst into a full belly laugh. "Woman, either you have more gall than the head of your household or . . . or you are possessed. Which is it?"

"May I re-cover his wound?"

"Yes, yes, go ahead." He realized the dirty trowel was still in his hand and tossed it aside. It clamored on the limestone floor. "Liars." He slowly turned completely around, hoping for someone's rebuttal. He pointed at Thaddaeus. "You. Do you know why we are really here?"

"No. Yes. You said yourself. You heard Mara and Peter arguing on the roof."

"Don't be stupid."

"Well, I . . . I—"

"We're here because we have been sent into this section of the city to find the other insurgents who came into Jerusalem with that one who was crucified yesterday. What was his name?" He looked at Peter. "And don't tell me you don't know his name. There were three crucified, but only one was crowned a King."

"His name was Jesus."

"Ah, yes. A Nazarene, that's right. Did you know him personally?"

The centurion's eyes bore into Peter's skull until Peter was forced to avert his gaze. "Me?"

"Yes. I'm talking to you."

Peter appealed for aid from among the helpless, sympathetic eyes. He ended his search when he confronted Mara's cold eyes. "Not . . . not personally."

"That's right," Andrew interrupted. "Nobody . . . nobody really knew him personally."

The centurion caught Mara's expression of disapproval. Then he shook his head. "Liar." He looked at Mara, again, expecting her to reveal something of the truth with her impulsiveness. But she proved to be disappointing to him with her continued silence. "Has anybody in here ever listened to his teachings?" Once again, the centurion scanned the room for an answer. A long silence taunted him instead. "What about a friend? Has anybody—"

"I've listened to his teachings," Mara submitted.

"Too bad," the centurion retorted.

"Why?"

"You're only a woman. Not worth the effort of an arrest."

"I can still think!" she shouted.

The centurion drew his long sword. "And I can easily take that away from you if you provoke me any further!"

Mara shot a hard glance at Peter, which did not escape the centurion's attention.

The centurion pointed the tip of his sword at Peter. "You. Step toward me."

Peter approached him until the tip of the sword was touching his chest.

The centurion was devoid of humor. "You did not have to know him personally to listen to his subversive teachings against Rome. Did you listen to his words?"

Peter looked helplessly at Andrew, who tried to support him with tender eyes.

"Answer me, damn you!" He pressed the sword against Peter's chest.

"I . . . I never . . . never heard his words, I swear!"

The centurion lowered his sword, came closer to Peter, then butted him on the side of his head with the handle of his sword.

Peter dropped to his knees from the blow; blood ran steadily down the side of his face from the gash in his temple.

"Liar. Judean liar!"

"He's a Galilean," Andrew remarked evenly.

The centurion approached him. "And you . . . you admit to be his brother?"

Hesitantly. "Yes."

"Ahh. Then that must make you a cowardly Galilean as well."

Andrew blinked his eyes several times to suppress his anxiety.

The centurion chuckled. "You people lack humor!"

"And you lack the effective execution of it," Mara challenged.

With both hands pressed against his bloody wound, Peter turned to her and hissed. "Mara, damn it: shut, your, mouth."

"You want effective execution, woman?" The centurion sauntered casually around Andrew. And after completing a full circle, the Roman kicked him in the gut.

Andrew's forearms flinched across his abdomen as he breathlessly hunched forward, paralyzed by the implosive power of the blow. He went down to his knees, unable to gasp for breath, and pressed his half-closed fists against his gut in a wretched display of helplessness.

Mara rushed to Andrew's assistance. "You animal! That served no purpose."

One of the legionnaires made a move to check her disrespect, but the centurion jerked his chin at him to keep the soldier from acting against her.

Mara's exploratory hands seemed to cause Andrew more distress; he pushed her away as he managed to inhale his first short breath.

She stood up and leveled her cold, steady eyes on the centurion. "How unclever."

The centurion was fully perplexed. He addressed Peter. "Now I'm certain: this woman of yours *is* possessed. I can see why you were having such an intense row with her." A couple of legionnaires chuckled. "Something tells me he's sleeping alone tonight."

Several of the legionnaires responded to the centurion's cue of levity by directing their amusement at Peter:

"Serves him right for marrying in the first place."

"I would have thrown her off the roof."

"A bachelor's life is the best way."

"You mean a soldier's life."

"With plenty of easy women and cheap wine."

"Steady, men."

"The centurion said steady!" the senior legionnaire shouted. The interior of the small dwelling became as silent as a tomb despite the numerous occupants.

The centurion turned to Peter again. "Get to your feet." Peter complied with some difficulty. "Take your hands from your face. You won't bleed to death." Peter lowered his arms. "Just look at that head wound, Sergeant. What do you think?"

"It's nothing but a scratch, sir. The most ordinary legionnaire could put in a full day's march after receiving that."

"Yes." The centurion set the point of his sword on the limestone floor and held it in front of him like a cane as he meticulously studied his captives:

The Galilean men were sweating with fear, while their women remained defiantly neutral. The Galilean boys were steadfast, but dismayed, while the willful girls suppressed their increasing trepidation.

Half the legionnaires in the room were growing bored, the other half were already indifferent to the centurion's method of terroristic interrogation.

"Galileans. Yes." An evil glint animated the centurion's face. He brought his sword to the ready and directed its point at Peter. "Surely, you were a follower of that man, Jesus."

The accusation struck horror in Peter's eyes.

"He was a Galilean, wasn't he? Wasn't he!"

"Yes!" Peter trembled before him.

"And Galileans always stick together—especially in Judea. So, it stands to reason that you must have known him—and known him well, right?" The centurion raised his sword as if he were going to cut Peter down. "Answer me!"

Peter dropped to his knees again, forgetting the pain of his head wound. "I . . . I don't know what you're saying, I don't know, I—"

Peter began to sob just as the centurion began to howl with cruel laughter. Their disharmony sent a chill through all of those at the centurion's mercy.

The Roman glanced at Mara's rigid figure. "You wanted humor?" he shouted toward what seemed to be on the edge of madness. "I'll show you humor!" He crowed once like an injured gamecock, then more loudly a second time.

The legionnaires laughed at his bizarre performance; it appeared that the centurion's animal imitation was related to some sort of inside barrack's joke.

The centurion watched Peter flatten into a prone position where he wept bitterly and uncontrollably into the palms of his hands. Then he sheathed his sword into his scabbard and waited for the laughter of his men to subside. "Palestine. Miserable, miserable Palestine. I'll be glad when I can wash its dust from my feet for the last time."

The senior legionnaire sidled over to his temperamental centurion and formally addressed him in an even voice. "Since this sector is clear, sir, shall I assemble the men?" The sergeant's steadfast professional bearing had a sobering effect on the centurion.

"Proceed."

The senior legionnaire raised his right fist above his head and made a firm circular gesture, which directed the soldiers to evacuate the dwelling. The sergeant was the last man to leave the irascible centurion amidst his Galilean audience.

The centurion listened to his men respond to the sergeant's call for line up and muster. The sound of this activity clearly gave him pleasure and a profound sense of meaning. Then he redirected his attention to the frightened inhabitants and quickly distilled the details of his visual impression into a single, overall feeling: the shallow breathing of public invisibility, which he'd grown to despise in this dismal place called Palestine. Aside from the pitiful man sobbing shamefully at his feet, even the haughty wench had withdrawn into reasonable caution. He was pleased with himself. "Fear Rome," he said. "That's the only certainty you need to know."

"Faith is more important than certainty," Mara offered.

"Ahh, so you do have a gentle side," the centurion quipped, before his facial expression darkened with severity. "You are lucky you said that to *me*, woman. Another centurion would have interpreted your remark as treasonous. I'll warn you only once: keep your beliefs to yourself. Besides, its magic obviously doesn't work."

As the centurion turned to leave, Peter grabbed him by his left foot. "Kill me, centurion. Kill me!"

The centurion was so startled that he pulled out a hidden dagger in self-defense. He shook his leg as if trying to free himself from a dog.

"Kill me! Please! There's nothing else for me to go on with after so much shame."

"Mad dog! Get away!" The centurion bent down and sliced the knuckles of Peter's right hand with his razor sharp blade. "Let go, I said." He kicked Peter in the face with his right foot and almost lost his balance. The centurion managed to stumble toward the doorway once he was free. "If that man wasn't possessed and if I weren't goodhearted, he would be on his way to his own crucifixion for assaulting a Roman officer."

The sergeant appeared smartly at the door. "All men are present and accounted for, sir." He regarded the dagger in the centurion's hand. "Is everything in order, sir?"

"Join the men. I'll be outside, momentarily."

"Yes, sir."

The centurion sheathed his dagger into a scabbard hidden behind him underneath his cloak. "You've been dealing with a kind viper. And, I assure you, if I'm ever required to return here, I'll show no leniency and offer no mercy."

"Please, please, please," Peter sobbed pitifully.

The centurion looked at the broken being on the ground. "This miserable creature is occupied by tormenting spirits. Cast him out before he infects all of you." He stepped through the opened doorway and joined his men outside.

The disciples listened to the centurion issue his next command. The smart stamp of their first step in unison signaled the departure of the formation. They waited with growing relief as the four squads of Roman soldiers marched away.

Thaddaeus dashed to the front doorway to verify what he was hearing. "They're really going."

Andrew hurried to his brother to comfort him. "Shut the door."

"What for?" Mara gibed. "The danger has passed."

Andrew glared at her. "Enough. That's enough out of you."

The harshness in his eyes and the severity in his voice alarmed Mara. She knew that her husband's brother was not a man to trifle with, especially at this very moment. She compressed her lips to display her quiet submission.

Thaddaeus shut the door. "Momentarily. The danger has passed only momentarily."

"Help me with Peter."

Thaddaeus crouched beside Andrew to help him lift Peter to his feet. Peter's face was swollen and bruised and the knuckles of his right hand were bleeding.

"Bring him over to this other pallet," Naomi said. "Mara, bring me a bowl of water. Miriam, cut some more linen."

The women went dutifully about their activities while Andrew and Thaddaeus assisted Peter to the pallet near Philip. Peter wrenched himself away from them, but stumbled and fell into a semiconscious state.

They dragged him back to that corner of the dwelling and rolled him onto his back into the pallet. Peter sank into a feverish delirium.

Andrew and Thaddaeus moved quickly away from him in order to give the women plenty of room to treat their second patient.

"We're coming apart," Andrew said. "Death and injury and constant fear is destroying us."

"Out of my way, Ira," said Naomi to her son. "Please, take your sister and Eli to the roof."

"But we're tired of the roof," Eli implored on Ira's behalf. But his true motive for resisting Naomi's suggestion surfaced with the increased proximity to his poor injured father. "Besides, he's . . . he's my father, no matter what. I'd like to help in any way I can."

"You're a very good son," Mara said sympathetically. She hugged him gently around the neck with her right arm. "But Naomi's right." She released him. "You, and the others, can help us by staying out of our way and—wait, better yet, feed the chickens and gather their eggs. There's always plenty to do if you can't amuse yourselves on the roof. Miriam, draw some water from the well. Ira, return those tools to the courtyard shed and, wait—there's milking to be done that's long overdue." Mara paused inwardly, in response to a tremor of melancholia. "Life's necessities must be attended to despite tragic events." Even though her voice had dropped to a whisper, everyone was listening intently. When she realized that all eyes were fixed on her, she became embarrassed by her vulnerable display of sentiment. "Leah, sweep out the

lower level there, especially near the repaired wall."
She clapped her hands briskly. "Come, come—let's get
to it! When you're done, perhaps the roof won't
appear to be so bad a place to be."

The interior of the dwelling became a beehive of
activity.

Naomi and Mara washed Peter's facial wounds and
wrapped his forehead with a white linen bandage to
cover the gash in his temple. They also wrapped his
right hand with a piece of clean linen to protect his
sliced knuckles. Meanwhile, Hanna continued to nurse
Philip, who seemed stable, though still hot with fever.

Thaddaeus nudged Andrew's side and whispered to
him as they observed the surrounding activity. "Perhaps
our coming apart is not so definite as you think."

"Perhaps," Andrew muttered. "But the source of
this present caregiving was almost the cause of our
destruction with that Roman. Although, in all fairness,
my brother has contributed a lion's share of misdeeds
lately."

"Still," Thaddaeus leaned closer to Andrew as he
cautiously scrutinized Mara. "Can't live with them,
can't live without them."

"I've avoided finding that out directly."

"Mara seems to be a pretty direct source of com-
parison for a bachelor like you."

"You can be sure of that, Thaddaeus. As I see it, my
sister-in-law is as direct a reflection on marriage as I'll
ever want to experience."

Both men suppressed their laughter. They shuffled
to the area where the breakfast mat had been spread

earlier, poured themselves some wine, and sat with their legs dangling over the ledge of the second floor level.

Peter caught a glimpse of Mara's stern expression through the corner of his right eye. He reached for his face with his left hand and stroked his thick beard before sinking back into semiconsciousness, which preceded another mental decline toward acute delirium:

Peter saw himself standing behind his Master, who was praying quietly under a tree. Peter stepped into its shade, but refrained from touching him. "Master, I know I'm forever asking you questions that seem to have no answers or . . . or, rather, have answers that forever escape my understanding. But Lord, where does forgiveness begin if I can't find forgiveness for myself? Forget my neighbor. What about me? How can I be forgiven, if I can't find it possible to forgive myself? And . . . and what is my own forgiveness worth without my own sacrifice? Speak to me, Rabbi. What is my sacrifice? Shall I—must I bear my own cross on some appointed day? What is my sacrifice? Will my courage fail me again at my appointed hour? Save me! What is my sacrifice? Save me! What is my meaning? Save me!" Peter shouted incoherently, as he sat up in his pallet trembling to the bone, soaked in a cold sweat.

Naomi was at his side trying to soothe him.

"Mara!" he shouted.

"This is Naomi."

"Mara. Mara, forgive me."

Naomi tried to calm him. "Please, lie down and get some rest."

"Philip? Where's Philip?"

"He's right behind you, sleeping. His fever broke during the last hour."

Peter craned his neck to see him. "Philip?"

"Easy there, he's going to be alright."

"Going to be, he's going . . . going to be—alright?" His eyes widened as if he suddenly understood the meaning of his words. "He's . . . he's alright?"

"Yes, yes, dear."

Peter began to hyperventilate with relief. "Are you sure?"

"Yes, yes—there, there. Lie down." Naomi pressed her hands against his powerfully built broad shoulders. "Rest, Peter."

He brushed her arms aside. "Where's Mara? Mara."

"She's gone."

"Then . . . then where's Eli? Eli?"

Naomi bit her lower lip. "She's taken Eli with her."

"Taken! Where?"

"She's gone, Peter. She's left you for good."

"But she can't leave me," he said soberly. "She's my wife. I can't and I won't give her a divorce."

"She's not seeking one."

Peter slumped forward.

"I'm sorry, Peter."

He rose from his pallet and stumbled backward on top of it like a confused stallion trapped in a stall. He steadied himself by pressing his right forearm against the wall. "How long have I been asleep?"

"Most of the day."

Peter scanned the interior. "Where is everybody?"

"Andrew and Thaddaeus went out to search for some of the others. Hanna took Ira and Leah with her to the market a little while ago. Miriam is on the roof repairing a mat."

"And my wife and boy are gone. Damn her for judging me."

"She said she was trying to come to terms with her new beliefs and with herself."

Peter stepped off the pallet, walked unsteadily past her, and kicked a pitcher that was set near the edge of the second floor ledge. He watched it smash against the hard dirt-packed ground floor. "What the hell does that mean, coming to terms?"

Naomi approached him without fear. "I don't know. But destroying other people's property won't give you the answer."

Peter jumped onto the lower floor to get away from her. "Women. You're all the same." Peter started for the open doorway, but stopped and turned toward Naomi instead of stepping through the door's threshold. "She'll change her mind."

"I wouldn't rely on that thought. It's over between you, she says. And there's nothing you can say to change her mind. You know Mara."

"Do I," he said sarcastically. He snorted. "Do I?" He paused introspectively. "She's too proud and heady for a woman."

"Blame that on Jesus. *Our* Jesus. He transformed me. Certainly, Mara. What did you expect? He spoke of the equality of the inner light, of the equality before God the Father. Do you think he didn't mean what he said? Did he not call us his disciples, as well? To him, we were not only partners, we were also contributors."

Peter sneered.

"Go ahead," she said. "Act like a man."

"How else should I act?"

"Better. Much better than you have been." Peter remained quiet with his shame as Naomi drifted into an inspired reverie. "It was in the course of our daily encounter with him, that each of us was shown a part of our new selves. Together, we represented a whole and a new kind of woman. Free to understand the spirit of his teachings. And, now, free to pass these teachings on to the seeker as best as we can without his physical presence."

"Bah. Wait until you face the real threat of the sword—or crucifixion—for yourselves. Then we'll see how bravely you'll speak."

"We suffer!"

"Agh, what form of demon possession is this?" Peter uttered with true bewilderment. "And you say this kind of thinking has actually spread among the other women, as well?"

Naomi was hesitant. "To some. In varying degrees. And according to their husband's tolerance."

"Then how come I was never made aware of this?"

"You weren't listening! Mara was as wide open to our Master's teachings as you were—and just as committed. She followed you into the beggar's road with him, didn't she? Admittedly, she was reluctant, at first. But she acquired a full-hearted commitment, after awhile. His miracles cast out her own demons of doubt and, in time, she was healing the sick with our Master's full approval. But you were too blind with ambition to see her good works."

"Ambition! There it is again," he muttered to himself. "Ambition?" Peter leaned against the doorjamb, staggered by the accusation. "Was I the only one not able to see my lust for power?" His chuckle was colored with irony. "Even worse: I thought I was wearing a clever disguise, but I was transparent to everybody—"

"And especially to our Master."

Peter lashed out viciously at Naomi. "You think I don't know that!"

"Finally, you know something!"

"You're beginning to behave like my wife."

"And my husband respects me for it."

"Your husband," he said contemptuously.

Naomi responded in a monotone for emphasis. "At least he had the courage to stand among the women at the foot of his cross."

Peter covered his ears with his hands. "Stop it, stop it! Everywhere I go I am tormented by this fact! Everyone I meet tells me it was John who stayed at his side. John—"

"My beloved husband: brave and fully tolerant of my open behavior."

"Then, I suppose, he approved of Mara."

"They got along well."

"I'm going out of my mind. No. My family thinks I've gone out of my mind. No. Demons. I must be occupied by demons. Oh, Master! Where are you when I need you the most?"

"You selfish rat. It's not only about your simple little public cowardice. It's about the kind of brute dominance you've displayed within our fold. You've transgressed with aggression against our own. The truth is, you're a troublemaker. You're a disciple who can't be trusted because he's been known to turn on his own people. Just look at Philip. My God, you almost killed him!"

"But . . . but I'm a peaceful man, I swear. Our Master, understood me. He knew I was hot-tempered."

Naomi shook her head dispassionately. "You don't get it. A peaceful man should maintain peace and kindness among his group—this gives us strength."

"Our Jesus was the peacemaker—"

"Who wanted us all to share the burden in order to protect the group. But you've never understood that. You have constantly relied on his forgiveness and his support to exonerate you time after time. But now—now that he's gone, there's nobody who'll defend your erratic behavior anymore. You're right. You've demons within you. And they keep growing stronger."

"Yes, that's right. That's right! They almost killed Philip. And I . . . I'm . . . I'm sorry."

"Mara has grown deaf to your apologies."

"And you?"

"I don't believe you," she uttered. "Your demons are still in you. And I'm sorry I provided you with an excuse."

"Bah—women."

"Oh how blind you are hiding behind demons. You're so deluded." She indicated the empty dwelling with the sweep of her right arm. "Do you see Andrew? Can you find Thaddaeus? And the others. Where are the others?"

"But I thought—you said that . . . that they were, I mean, Andrew and—"

"*They* had enough of you. True, Andrew and Thaddaeus are roaming the city looking to make contact with the others—"

"But my brother *and Thaddaeus* denied Jesus before that centurion, as well. They denied him!"

"Mara doesn't care about what they've done or haven't done."

"Bah!"

"And the truth is, I don't care either."

"But why should my failures have any more significance than theirs?"

"Because your actions have been . . . have been cumulative; your deeds have been building upon themselves for quite some time. Like I said, you and your anger, your relentless dominance, your . . . your aggression among us has proved you to be undesirable—even dangerous."

"But . . . but they denied him," Peter said meekly.

"To be afraid is not a crime among us. They are suffering with their own form of self-contempt." Her tone hardened. "But they're not assaulting their loved ones every time they are faced with their own shortcomings, unlike you who causes pain through word and deed and worse: because your destruction is more devastating to the community *by virtue* of your powerful and sought-after position."

"By virtue, you say—*some virtue*," he lamented with self-pity. "This dark virtue of mine has left me condemned."

"No. You're still loved despite your contemptible behavior. It's just, well, none of us knows how to deal with you any longer. Without Jesus, you are, well, you're simply a menace. And since we will not submit to the rule that blood demands blood, then you must be cast out from us before it's too late."

"Jesus would never have allowed that."

"He's no longer with us."

"He said he would return."

"He said a lot of things."

Peter raised his head like a howling dog. "Jesus! Where are you! I need you!"

Peter dashed through the open doorway and ran into the narrow street. His wild eyes frightened a young woman burdened by a large jug of water. Peter stretched his arms toward her to indicate that he was harmless, as well as to steady his nerves. "Don't be afraid." He pressed his back against the nearby wall behind him to demonstrate his harmlessness. "Please, pass. Please. I'm not dangerous."

The woman scampered by him, keeping as much distance from the madman as the narrow street would allow.

Peter closed his eyes. "My God, my God, what am I going to do?" He pushed himself away from the wall and ran down to one end of the street where he stopped at the intersection to study the activity in the wider thoroughfare. An abstract haze clouded the periphery of his vision, and the direct sunlight forced him to squint.

Several pedestrians veered toward the opposite side of the street to avoid him. A man riding a donkey flicked the beast's rump to speed past him. Another man glared suspiciously at him from atop his perch as he guided his ox-drawn cart toward its destination with a long prodding-pole.

Peter's paranoia increased proportionately to the amount of stares he received by passing strangers. His bandaged head and hand, his bruised and battered face, his torn tunic must have been the reason he was drawing so much attention, he reasoned. He debated whether to return to Aaron's dwelling, but decided against it.

He stepped into the busy Jerusalem street and followed its flow deeper into the lower city.

The heavy mud was inescapable until he reached a roughly paved thoroughfare clogged with people and animals. He almost ran into a woman carrying her son on her shoulders. He backed away from her and almost collided with a farmer's wife who had flat cakes of dung stacked and balanced on her head. He swerved away from her just in time, then quickly sidestepped a porter bent over by the heavy burden of wood he had strapped across his back and shoulders.

"Out of my way, you!" the porter demanded.

Peter dodged the man and quickly shifted around

to avoid the oncoming traffic, then turned into its engulfing flow. He moved with its current, not knowing how else to solve his disorientation, and went deeper into the lower end of the city, where the filth of poverty was greater and the living conditions were frightfully insufficient.

He wandered aimlessly in this region like a hungry ghost. The only thing that was certain was the approach of sunset.

Music and tambourines, dancing and laughter filled the narrow street as outside oil lamps twinkled brightly in the dusk. Peter had stumbled into a wedding party, which seemed to have been in process all day despite the weather. Most of the party was taking place inside the largest dwelling on that street. And although most of the feasting and festivities remained indoors, some of the celebrants meandered outside for some fresh air during this break in the weather.

Peter stood in the periphery of the party feeling more abstract by the gaiety of the laughter and food-filled chatter. He began to back away and retrace his steps when an elderly man approached him.

"It appears as if you could use a drink, my friend."

"I could use many," Peter said.

"Then come dance with us."

The elderly man was almost half Peter's size and stoop-shouldered, as well. His thick beard was grey and his eyes were blue. His head was covered with a bleached clean linen, wrapped around his head several times into a handsome turban. He wore a long outer robe with wide open sleeves over an inner striped tunic made of silk. The old man's expensive attire and scrupulous grooming forced Peter to consider his reduced and wretched appearance. He was hurt and bruised, and his clothes were dirty and torn.

"No, I can't. Look at me." He pointed to the bandage around his forehead. "Not exactly a gentleman's turban. I can't join you in this terrible condition." Peter began to leave.

"It's obvious to me that this is not your usual physical or mental state. You're not a common beggar."

"No." Peter grinned. "Not common."

"This is my brother-in-law's wedding party for his youngest. Come. Join me. You'll be my special guest. The procession to fetch the bride took place several days ago and the marriage has been successfully consummated. Everyone has eaten their fill for days and the drinking—oh, the drinking. Believe me, you'll hardly be noticed."

For once, Peter kept quiet and allowed the kind old man to lead him into his fold where he was greeted without too many questions or sidelong glances from this Egyptian clan.

The bowl of water provided for him to wash his feet and hands was quickly replaced with a cup of wine and a space that brought him within reach of richly prepared food.

Peter ate little. His poor disposition in the wake of his recent series of spiritual and moral failures prevented him from joining in the festivities. To the depths of his soul, he was sick of deception, sick of appearing to be someone he was not. He had failed his Master, his brethren, and himself in every conceivable manner. And, now, he was being comforted by a kindly stranger and his family.

This was the sort of behavior that his Master had sought to instill in him through his many examples and patient teachings. But he had not been bright enough to be a good student.

The elderly man gently nudged Peter. "You're thinking too much when it should be a time to release yourself of your inner burden."

"Who are you?" Peter inquired, full heartedly. "Why should you care about my lack of joy?"

"I'm nobody. And call this friendly treatment an old man's extravagance." He indicated the surrounding festivities with the sweep of his arm. "In a world wracked by so much suffering, sometimes a man must find a way to ease some of the general pain. Today, I've chosen to pay attention to somebody else's pain— yours, a nameless being from a humble station in life. Although my family has managed to prosper more than those who surround us, we have managed not to forget where we've come from."

Peter drank deeply from his cup. "You speak so easily about generosity and kindness—traits that have been hard-won for me, then lost, time and time again."

"Drink. Try to be merry." Then the old man introduced Peter to several key members of the family before departing his company.

In a short time, the rich wine went to Peter's head by way of his empty stomach. Without his awareness, the music became sweeter sounding, the laughter became less piercing, and the dancing appeared moderately grotesque.

He increased his drinking and, conversely, decreased his perceptions. Everything became a blur of movement and sound and light. In an effort to cast away his memory, he cast away his ability to be social. The final thing he clearly remembered was his last failure: to show gratitude and respect toward the old man and his clan.

Peter felt two strong arms hook under his armpits and the next thing he discerned was the smell of the night air. The men on either side of him were firm, but not harsh.

He knew his feet were dragging on the hard-packed dirt ground, even though he couldn't feel them. He knew he'd been tossed to the ground, even though he never felt the impact. Words had been spoken to him or at him or about him, but only one word had been heard: "ungrateful."

He lifted his face from the damp street and heard the men depart. Then he turned his head to his left and vomited before he turned it to his right and passed out.

CHAPTER 3

The Lamentation

Peter heard their presence.

"What have we got here?" one of them said as the other man nudged Peter's side with a cautious foot.

The unwanted tactile encounter awakened the full, miserable extent of Peter's aching body. The sliced knuckles of his linen-wrapped right hand throbbed, and the deep gash to his left temple intensified the pain of his hangover.

"What kind of turban is that?"

"It isn't. It's a head bandage."

"Ahh. Wounded. A brawl?"

"No doubt. His face is beaten and bruised."

"And his tunic is in shreds."

"He's no beggar. He's seen too many meals. Besides, look at him. His is not a beggar's attitude."

"Or physique."

"A deserter, you think?"

"Nah. There's no sign of a legionnaire in this one."

"He's a grizzly sort."

"Still."

One of them knelt beside Peter.

"What are you doing, Ganto?"

"I can't help myself."

"You can't help every misfortunate character in Palestine."

Ganto scratched his beard. "I recognize this one, Halab."

"Ahh, that's different." Halab stooped alongside Ganto for a closer study of the semiconscious man.

Peter stirred.

"Look, the poor dumb creature is coming back to life."

Peter rolled to his side and squinted at the daylight. Then he gazed at the nearby men. "I'm not afraid of you."

"There's no reason to be."

Peter licked his cracked lips and swallowed hard to moisten the back of his throat. His husky voice still broke. "I'm not Judas."

"That's right."

"Judas?" Halab inquired. "Who's that?"

"Nobody you need to know about. Let's help this one against the wall."

They coaxed Peter to sit up, then lifted him by his

armpits toward a close-by wall and leaned him against it for back support.

"Bah. He stinks of ammonia."

Peter's dirty woolen tunic clung heavily to his wet skin. His long hair shagged outward from under his linen head-wrap in all directions, his thick unkempt beard gave him the appearance of being a man who was occupied by several demons, and his feet and sandals were caked with mud of varying degrees of dryness.

Halab cautiously squatted to Peter's right side and glanced at Ganto, who remained standing to Peter's left. "Look at this poor dumb creature."

"I can see him well enough from where I'm standing."

"Who gave you this beating?"

Peter snarled. "None of your business."

"Ho! Listen to him!"

"Where am I?"

"You tell us," said Ganto.

Peter pressed the back of his head against the wall and searched his memory for the immediate past. Darkness enveloped him once again, but his mind continued to struggle for some degree of recollection.

As if aroused from another dream, he suddenly reawakened from the drunken state of unconsciousness he had incurred from the wedding party.

He remembered being dragged to the end of an alley, where he was left swimming in his vomit; he remembered rising to his feet sometime thereafter, where he feebly groped about in Jerusalem's dark, vacant streets until he stumbled onto a violent scene:

There were two against one. Both men were bigger than their victim who was begging for mercy. Where the source of light came from was unknown, but Peter saw the momentary glint of a dagger before it plunged downward and disappeared into the silhouette of the victim. The cry, followed by a throat-cutting gurgle, sent a chill through Peter, which forced him to call out to them.

"Halt! You there! What's going on?" he shouted, using an official tone which startled and frightened both assailants. Peter's size and aggressive approach forced them to flee into the dark maze of the city's streets.

Peter ran to the victim to give him assistance, but it was too late. Upon closer inspection, he discovered that the stabbed man had died from a slit throat. He knelt beside the body, more from exhaustion than from added curiosity, and touched the man's left arm for confirmation. The skin was clammy, the bare arm was limp. As soon as he released the arm, he noticed the bulge underneath the breast of the victim's tunic. He slipped his left hand underneath the man's collar and fished out a heavy leather purse. He untied and opened it and verified its contents: shekels and denarii. He quickly retied the neck of the purse and slipped it underneath the breast of his own tunic where it dropped into the void above his waist strap. He stood up, stepped over the growing puddle of blood, and ran until he stumbled breathlessly against a wall. Without reason or notice, he began to cry.

The weight of the purse against his lower breast felt

like the burning pressure of a growing tumor. He reached inside his tunic, wrenched the searing object from his breast, and sought to throw it as far into the darkness as he could when he was startled by a seductive voice. Peter did not hear her words, only her cautious tone: a pitch usually reserved for calming domestic animals, beasts of burden, dogs.

She appeared to be in a bad way herself: dirty, ragged, gaunt by chronic hunger. Only her sparkling dark eyes conveyed the past glory of her beauty. Her attempt to sashay toward him failed because of several clumsy missteps caused by mud holes and ruts; her voice, although still alluring, rasped desperately toward the edge of dissonance. "Hello there."

"Who are you?"

"What does it matter?"

"Nobody lives in this kind of darkness."

"You call this living?"

"This is not a dream."

"Two nobodies on an empty street is a sad reality. And so is that purse you have in your hand."

Peter presented the purse to her. "Take it."

"Now that's not reality."

"It feels very solid in my hand."

"But what goes with it?" The woman noticed his confused expression. "What must I do to earn so much weight?"

Peter looked at the purse, then extended his arm with an emphatic gesture. "Take it."

"I have a price."

"I'm giving you all I have!"

"That's not enough in exchange for all that I have left."

"And that is?"

"My self-respect."

"A woman in your profession—"

"Can still possess pride!" She grimaced. "I see you're not as virginal as I mistook you for."

"I've never bought a woman's favor."

"And I've never imposed a precondition. It seems we're even." The woman stepped closer to him and placed her hand on the purse. "I'll not take all of this."

"Take it all," he insisted.

"No." She took the purse and carefully slipped it back inside the breast of his tunic in a manner that established an intimacy between them. "I know of a place where we can eat and drink beforehand, a place where we can be safe and dry for a little while. That's reality."

She led him through an endless series of dark backstreets until they came to a large structure with heavy shutters against its two windows and a set of double doors protecting its main entrance. Inside, there was light and warmth, food and drink and, eventually, naked companionship on a dirty straw pallet in a back room, which became more sordid and, God help him, more stimulating when he saw her spit in her hand, then moisten herself between her legs. It all happened so quickly and surreptitiously that, if the weight of his purse hadn't been reduced by half to verify the experience, it surely would have been a dream caused by the consumption of too much wine along with the destruction of his self-respect.

Peter opened his eyes when he felt a hand press against the tumor in his chest.

"Where are you?" Ganto asked.

Peter brushed Halab's hand aside. "Get away."

"We're not here to rob you!" Halab said indignantly. "You'd have been dead already if that were our intention."

Peter studied Halab with one eye closed. "You've a Syrian accent."

"That's right." Halab shared a grin with Ganto. "What of it?"

Peter did not answer, but continued studying the man who was plagued by boils on the face, as well as behind the neck and ears. The Syrian's scraggly beard could not cover his dark and pock-marked facial landscape. His thick, wavy, black hair came down to his short, powerful neck and framed a pair of black eyes.

Peter turned to Ganto. "Who is this Syrian?"

"A deserter. Like the rest of us."

Peter rubbed his aching forehead. "What's his cause?"

"I had enough of Rome," Halab answered for himself.

"We all have."

"But I deserted from the Auxiliary Legions."

"Why?"

"One too many injustices. The harshness of an unfair centurion can break any man."

Peter sought Ganto's confirmation with a quizzical facial expression, which Ganto chose to ignore. Ganto's formidable presence, iron-hard body, and sharp disposition made Peter cautious. He knew Ganto by reputation: a capable and ruthless brigand chief who had earned the confidence of countless poor and hungry peasants because of his deep sense of justice. Ganto was also stout and brutish, like Halab. Both men wore clean, knee-length tunics and leather sandals. But unlike Halab's uncovered shaggy head, Ganto wore a linen turban and possessed a full and well-shaped beard.

Ganto reached under Peter's armpit. "Give me a hand with him, Halab."

Together, they helped Peter to his unsteady feet.

"So, what does this one do?"

"Him?" Ganto studied Peter with an expression of amusement painted across his face. "He's a disciple to a dead prophet."

"Huh?"

"Crucified. You know. The one from Nazareth that Rome executed a couple of days ago."

"Ahh, the king."

"His name is Jesus," said Peter.

"Was, my sick-looking friend. Was."

Halab laughed at Ganto's pitiless statement. "Didn't he claim to be related to one of our gods?"

"He claimed nothing, pagan."

Halab released Peter's arm in response to Peter's snide remark. "Be careful, Galilean. Your . . . your Yahweh is nothing but a storm god, a rider on the clouds. Besides, we all sacrifice the same animals."

"You employ prostitutes, not priests."

Halab shoved Peter. "Roman gods are as good as any. And all burnt offerings look the same, Hebrew."

"Even Syrian?"

"You provoke me further and I'll show you how a conquered people can fight. Just because every Semite nation has trampled on Syria doesn't mean I have to listen to the ravings of a Galilean."

"You obviously listen to him," Peter challenged, referring to Ganto.

"Flow with it, Galilean," said Halab, deciding to be reasonable. "You are a conquered people, as well."

"I'll never accept Roman rule."

"Learn more Greek."

"Like you?" Peter said facetiously.

Halab jutted his proud chin toward him. "Damn right. As well as Hebrew, Latin, Aramaic, and Syriac. Although," he nudged Ganto in an attempt at good humor, "I can't read or write a word in any of them!" Halab laughed heartily as Ganto chuckled.

"Not surprising," Peter said callously. "And Syriac the last on your list."

Halab's laughter ended abruptly. "What is this, Ganto? This Galilean is beginning to try my patience." He stepped nose to nose with Peter. "I said learn more Greek. Herod is bent on Hellonizing Palestine."

"Never happen."

"My life in Damascus as an Auxiliary Legionnaire really wasn't so bad. Flow with it."

"Like you, Syrian?"

"Yes. Well. But I was doing alright there for awhile, but then, well . . . like I said, I had to desert."

"Typical."

Halab's serious anger was smoldering to the surface. "I've killed once because of uncontrolled anger.

And now that I have nothing to lose, believe me, I can kill again."

"Is that a threat?" Peter leaned his face closer to Halab's.

"I never threaten. Ganto, this one is either fearless or as stupid as a rock."

"Whoa, you two. Easy. Easy!" Ganto's voice was firm and authoritative. "There are plenty of enemies surrounding us to fight. Direct your anger at them."

"He started it!"

"I suggest you steer away from our differences or I'll be forced to draw my dagger," Halab threatened.

"Alright, enough, I said," Ganto ordered. "Easy there, Halab. And you," he released Peter's arm, "shut up. We, that is, Jews and Syrians have fought each other enough in the past. Let's bury our differences for now—among us, at least." He grinned at Halab. "Besides, who gives a damn about the past, right?"

Halab expressed his reluctant agreement by shaking his head before he addressed Peter. "Believe in your god and I'll believe in mine."

"Or none at all," Ganto added.

The remark caught Halab off guard. "Ho. Ha ha! Right! You're a real one, Ganto. Nothing fake about you." He turned to Peter as he continued to refer to Ganto. "Straight up and down he is, my friend. Straight up and down." Halab studied Peter. "Well, at least this one has a bite and a willingness to show his teeth. I respect that. I respect that a lot!"

"So do I," Ganto said before addressing Peter. "Are you able to travel?"

Peter took several unsteady steps. "Sure. Where to?"

"Well, first, you look as if you need a drink."

Peter ran his left hand through his hair. "I don't know. I feel awful."

"All the better. Hair of the dog treatment is what you need."

"And judging by the bulge in your purse," Halab augmented, "you can afford it."

Peter shook his head. "Alright."

"Good," Halab said gleefully. "You've a lousy disposition, but a generous purse. That evens things out as far as I'm concerned."

Peter patiently rolled his eyes. "I'm glad you think so."

"Ho. Ho, ho! I think you just attempted your first piece of humor." Halab slapped him on the back. "Good for you. Good for you. And as soon as we get something to eat and drink, we'll take you with us."

"Where to?"

Halab glanced at Ganto conspiringly. "To triple the money in your purse!"

"How are you going to do that?" Peter said to Halab while seeking his answer from Ganto by the projected apprehension in his eyes.

"Relax, Peter," said Ganto. "He's only referring to a cockfight. Come on. You've nothing more to lose. And, quite frankly, nothing else to do."

The streets were deformed by the hardened ruts that were formed by cart wheels grinding through the mud during the last two days of intermittent rain. Everything was damp: clothes and straw, walls and beasts. And with the sun's increased intensity, the humidity rose from water puddles, standing sewage, and overflowed cisterns. Mud wall cave-ins were rampant, leaving households temporarily exposed to the public streets.

The stench of damp wool reeked from the clothes of the homeless and from the unfortunate pilgrims unable to find adequate shelter the night before. In general, the discomfort from the late season's heavy rain caused the expression of stoicism to prevail on the multitudes of Jerusalem's inhabitants.

Marketplaces were crammed with lethargic travelers and occupied with more merchants, traders, and peddlers than standing customers. Traders waited anxiously in their booths for the beggars to clear out and for the paying customer to finally stop and shop and forget the discomfort of the city's streets.

The congestion in the city seemed more stifling by the low overcast of the sandy-gray sky that appeared solid to the eye, and the windless humidity made everything stick to itself, especially wool to skin.

The main thoroughfares were crowded with arriving travelers and departing caravans and the reverse; it was difficult to discern, from the hectic activity, which was which and for whom it was the end of the Passover festival. By closely following Halab and Ganto toward this recommended establishment for their morning repast, Peter was able to avoid direct contact with his tumultuous surroundings. All was a whirling blur of color and a deafening mixture of sound, which occasionally presented itself in some distinct manner: a lost boy crying for his mother, a beggar pleading his woe, a musician singing for coin, an aggressive merchant hollering "Figs for sale!"

Peter's headache grew worse, and his desire to reach their destination increased in direct proportion to the throb of his hangover.

The collision was sudden, unprovoked, and head on: the smaller man stumbled backward and fell.

"Watch where you're going," Peter grumbled, knowing it was as much his own fault as the other man's. Peter started to walk past the small man when he noticed that only the whites of his eyes were visible. He was blind and old and dressed in rags. And although the man was also having difficulty getting to his feet, Peter hurried past him rather than offer him assistance or alms, which he could have afforded. Instead, Peter exaggerated his pace to demonstrate his need to keep up with his two guides; it was a performance motivated by guilt and aimed to disassociate himself from the incident.

The blind man never uttered a word, but somehow managed to keep his useless white eyes trained on Peter until the space between them filled up with people.

Peter called out to Ganto and Halab and asked them to wait for him in an effort to publicly exonerate himself and erase some of the effect of his guilt. It was a cheap act of justification that made him feel smaller than the hapless man he left behind. This overruling shame, however, made him stop and consider turning around to offer the blind man some assistance. But Ganto's impatient call for him to quicken his pace forced Peter to discard the thought; he scurried sheepishly toward his unknown destination.

In his effort to catch up to Ganto and Halab, who veered right at an intersection and disappeared from his sight, Peter carelessly sprinted after them. He stumbled, ankle deep, into a mud puddle and plopped onto his hands and knees for a ridiculous finale. Peter heard laughter before he had time to explode with anger. He raised his head and saw Halab and Ganto leaning against a wall of a two-story structure near the turn of the street corner.

"Very funny," Peter said.

"From where we're standing, you're hilarious."

"You'd have made an excellent clown at the Roman circuses."

Peter stood up and, as he flung the mud from his hands, pedestrians swerved to avoid him.

Their laughter increased when they saw Peter walk out of his sandals because of the mud's suction.

"Damn!"

"My, my, isn't he temperamental?" said Halab.

"Are you two going to take me to a clean dry place to eat and drink or not?"

Ganto pointed at a door to his right. "Over there. Across that street is our destination. Come on." Ganto stepped into the street, with Halab in tow, and waited for his pitiful companion to join them. "You can wash up inside. They'll be expecting men in your condition."

Halab guffawed. "And don't forget your sandals. You're going to need your sandals."

Peter wrenched them out of the mud and followed them into the comfort of the establishment without uttering another word.

They lounged on a long bench that was pushed against a wall for back support. All three men had washed up, then eaten and drunk their full. The Roman-style tavern was clean, airy, and late-morning quiet. A glassy-eyed contentment dominated their expressions and kept their conversation friendly.

"Nobody forced me to join the Legions," Halab said philosophically. "There was simply no other way to make a living. In fact, I saw real combat because I volunteered for the German wilderness. I wanted my fair chance at capturing some plunder, which I did—but, well, I lost it all throwing dice." He frowned, then drank half the wine from his cup. "Oh well, can't take it with you." He shook his head to regain his mental clarity, then focused his attention on Peter. "Anyway, I just made the standard for height, though my physical strength surpassed most recruits." He raised his powerful hand toward Peter. "Take it. See how powerful I am."

Peter brushed Halab's arm away. "Go on, I believe you."

Halab looked at his muscular arm and smiled. "Made of iron."

"No doubt."

Halab thumped himself on the chest with pride. "I was lucky. I was recruited, given advanced pay, and posted without a letter on my behalf." He inhaled, then exhaled grandiosely. "I was recruited based on my interview and my strength."

Peter glanced at Ganto. "Good."

"After giving my military oath, I was tattooed with the military mark and dispatched to my unit with a group under the charge of a draft officer."

"He was lucky," Ganto interjected.

"That's right," said Halab. "I was lucky. I was sent to a good auxiliary force in Syria where I trained with the XVI Flavia Legion. That meant hard professional training, which saved my life many times over when I was later transferred to an auxiliary force attached to XIII Gemina in the Rhineland."

"The one you volunteered for?"

"That's right," said Halab, pleased by Peter's attentiveness. "This one listens, Ganto. I like that." He winked at Peter. "You know, Ganto would have done well in the legions."

"Bah! Roman structure is not for me." Ganto drained his cup of wine and waited for the other two to do the same before ordering a refill.

Peter studied his freshened cup of wine. "Was training hard?"

"Oh, yes," said Halab, as he caressed his cup with both hands. "And dangerous. There was marching, physical training, swimming, and gladiatorial weapons training." He shook his head gravely. "Yes, everybody was carefully trained at the stakes with heavy shields and swords—but made of wood, at first, and twice the weight of the real weapons." He rested his chin under the heel of his right hand in an attitude of recollection. "That six-foot stake in the ground was my enemy for a long, long time. We learned to strike with the point, you see, not with the edge."

"And after the stake?"

"With each other, of course."

"What happened to those who failed to reach the standard of combat required?" asked Ganto.

"Those who failed received their rations in barley instead of wheat until they passed the practical tests. The senior officers were usually pretty hard on them at this point."

"I bet."

"The same method of instruction was used in training with a pilum." Halab exhaled deeply for emphasis before drinking some of his wine. "The weight of that training javelin was a killer. And, and don't forget, in addition to weapons training, we continued with daily arms drill, physical training, and marching. We even practiced throwing stones up to a litra in weight."

"Sounds tough."

"That's not the long of it, Peter. As soon as we acquired these individual skills, the drill masters combined them all into a single fluid proficiency."

"I agree with Ganto. There's too much structure in that training."

"Hell," Halab boasted, "that was only basic training. Field service training soon followed."

"What's the difference?"

Halab leaned toward Peter like an instructor. "Field service means marching in full order."

"What's that?"

"A long routed march with the weight of arms, equipment, and rations."

"Like beasts of burden," Ganto qualified.

"Exactly. The loads were heavy. And constant practice in preparation for strenuous campaigns was necessary, according to those in command." Halab nodded his head to increase the significance of his words. "This led us to severe field training, which consisted of daily camp construction and camp fortification. It was backbreaking work of the lowest form: digging ditches, fixing palisades, constructing ballista platforms, and building up low internal banks of turf for shelter tents—endless, it was endless work and harsh discipline." Halab grinned. "But I liked it. Men of strength always liked it. Y–e–s," he boasted, "my unit's officers were hard to approach and grudging with favors. They were strict and conscientious about regulations and, for some time, even forbade camp followers, merchants, and soothsayers from our midst. We slept on the ground, ate plain boiled regulation food, and always marched, never rode the pack mules; we lived under canvas in winter and summer, no matter the harshness of the weather. Y–e–s, it was a privilege to serve with those warriors."

"Were there deserters?" Peter asked.

Halab drank some wine and wiped his lips with the back of his arm. "Not many. Those who abandoned the colors were usually caught." He lowered his gaze in Ganto's direction and spoke gravely. "They paid for their error at once with their lives."

"The poor slobs," said Ganto. "Everything, concerning Rome, is always a matter of life and death," he added bitterly.

"I'll drink to that," said Peter.

"Here, here." Halab clinked his cup against Peter's, then Ganto's, before draining it to the bottom. "Another round, what do you say?"

Peter agreed, and Ganto gestured to the tavern keeper for more wine.

"Sounds like a bore," said Peter as he watched the tavern keeper refill his cup. "All that marching and digging sounds like a bore."

"Our training in battle formations was far more interesting," Halab reassured. "Learning to keep your allotted position in line required constant practice when commanded to go from a single line to a double line or to go from the square to the wedge. I know for a fact that practice in these movements taught us to keep our ranks during real fighting. Even if our ranks had been broken by the enemy, there was the circle formation in retreat to prevent a mass rout."

Ganto belched from the wine he'd just drunk. "Sounds as if you saw a lot of combat."

"If only that were true." Halab leaned back against the wall. "Most of our duties were devoted to peacekeeping duties, which meant numerous fatigues."

"What's that?" asked Peter.

"Fatigues." Halab grimaced. "Cleaning latrines and baths, building roads and fort repair, guard duty, line and road patrol, general housekeeping and armory duties and a whole multitude of other jobs that were more civilian in nature. Fatigues." He drank some wine as if he were trying to wash out a bad taste in his mouth. "That's what eventually got me into trouble."

"Civilian work," Ganto said with sympathy.

"Yes. Plain and ordinary. *And* the bullshit associated with an unreasonable prick of a centurion not half the soldier that I was. Bah! The bastard deserved my dagger to the heart. I was immune," he lamented, "exempt from general duty: fatigue. I'd earned my position as a workshop sergeant the hard way. But when that bastard took my rank away and ordered me to cut building-stones, I had enough. Out came my dagger and, well, now I'm an enemy of Rome."

"And a friend of mine," Ganto added. He glanced at Peter. "You're in good company. We're all enemies of Rome."

"Not by choice," Peter countered.

"No matter. If caught, you'll be crucified like a common criminal."

"Yes," Halab said bitterly. "Born common and common we shall die."

Ganto slapped Halab warmly on the back. "You're still a warrior."

"I'll drink to that."

"And one of the best under my command."

"You know I'm dependable where profit is concerned."

"Right. And that's the only kind of profit to follow." Ganto turned to Peter. "Right?"

Peter swallowed hard. He would not respond to Ganto's twisted humor.

Ganto nudged him with his elbow. "Good. At least you're not angry."

Peter nodded. "Yes. At least."

They were very high, bordering on drunk. Their conversations had drifted from one subject to another and into casual intimacies that bordered on trust. And like so many conversations among Palestinian men in the past two days, their conversation finally reached the political question concerning the one who'd been crucified for being a king among the Jews.

"Earthly deliverance," Halab said with a slur in his speech. "Your anointed one should have at least offered you earthly deliverance."

Peter pressed his thick lips together thoughtfully before attempting to respond. "He had heavenly qualities—"

"To what end?" Ganto interrupted heavily.

"I . . . he . . . he was the Messiah."

"Bah!" Ganto belched with disgust. "Have it your way."

"You don't believe me."

"I know what I saw," Halab said. "A dead man nailed to the wood."

"He . . . he was one with the Father."

"Not mine," said Ganto. "And if so, what of it?"

"He will rise again. I'm sure of it."

Halab glanced at Ganto to share his puzzlement, then decided to humor Peter. "By what means? And why?"

176

"I . . . I don't know how—"

"Death and resurrection. Ha!" Ganto motioned at the tavern keeper to refill their cups. "Nice trick if he can do it. Damn, I'd certainly be impressed with that performance."

"He'd certainly have a full collection purse over that bit of magic," Halab agreed.

"He will rise, in earnest, I tell you, and proclaim to me his intent. This will be my—our—salvation."

"Bah! You had it right the first time, Peter—your salvation, not ours."

Both men chuckled at Peter without venom.

Peter looked broodingly into his cup as the tavern keeper refreshed it with more wine. He waited until all three cups were charged before he spoke. "Sin. Death. Salvation. At what point do they meet? And why? What did he mean to do at their juncture?"

Halab peered at Ganto and raised his eyebrows. "Who?"

"His Master, Jesus, of course. The anointed one."

"Ah." Halab pursed his lips before he spoke to Peter. "You ask impossible questions. You expect too much from this so-called anointed—"

"Not so-called."

Halab raised both hands into the air in a gesture of innocence. "Fine. *The* anointed one." He chuckled, reducing Peter's certainty to doubt by his display of amusement.

Peter drank heavily from his cup, which inspired the other two to do the same. "Both of you think I'm a fool, don't you?"

Halab slapped Peter on the back to soothe him. "Nah! Just fool–ish. It's the wine speaking . . . for all three of us."

"I'm not drunk."

"Then you should be, my new friend. Let's drink up and eliminate any doubt over our sobriety."

"I'll drink to that," Ganto said with increased amusement. He peered at Peter as he referred to Halab. "He's truly alright, for a Syrian."

Halab also peered at Peter as he referred to Ganto. "And he's alright, for a Jew."

Ganto raised his cup of wine. "To your health."

Halab raised his cup, as well. "May your health increase beyond measure. Come on, Peter, forget our differences. And forget that stuff about," he looked at Ganto, "what was that he was saying?"

"Salvation."

"Yes, yes, whatever that is. Drink up!"

Peter raised his cup with great physical effort and with an equal determination of the mind. He even smiled. "Yes, you're right. And yes, I'm not drunk—yet."

"Ha, ha! That's the spirit," Halab chortled. "That's the spirit!"

But the very thing lacking in Peter's eyes was spirit. He drank deeply to keep up with Halab and Ganto, as well as to leave behind some of his torment. He even forced himself to laugh aloud, but his cohorts were not convinced of his joy.

The three of them stumbled through the streets of Jerusalem; their speech was slurred and their vision was off-centered.

"Do you mean to tell me that you, a fully grown man, have never been to a cockfight? Ganto, what kind of friend is this you've introduced me to?"

"He wasn't a friend at all. Merely, an acquaintance—until now, right Peter?"

"I . . . I suppose there's . . . there's something right about that."

The three of them dissolved into an uncontrolled bout of silly laughter inspired by too much drink as they continued toward their destination. And when the sun suddenly peered through a crack in the clouds, it forced them to squint and grunt with greater effort.

"A cockfight," Peter mumbled in dismay. "I still can't believe you two are taking me to a cockfight."

"Relax," Halab said with assurance. "You're going to love it. It's a place where life meets death on its own terms. You'll see. You'll see."

They proceeded along narrower and narrower streets toward the far edge of the poorest section of the city. The sky was still uncharacteristically gray despite the harsh glint of the sun.

As they wound their way through the labyrinth of humble streets into a remote section of Jerusalem, the presence of women and their domestic activities became more dominant. In addition, the metropolitan flavor of the city weakened with each turn of a corner. It was as if they'd disappeared into a countryside village where the mundane tasks of ordinary living prevailed.

They heard their destination before they reached it. The sound of men contained into a restricted area had a distinctive sound to it.

"That's it, over there," Halab said. "They haven't started yet."

"How can you tell? Damn. You can hear them from here," said Peter.

"If you think they're loud now," Ganto warned, "wait until the blood begins to flow."

"Right. And the true wagering begins," Halab added. "Passions run high when a blood sport is enhanced by the gain and loss of money. Yes, blood, it's . . . it's a powerful force."

When they reached a heavy gate, which led into an outdoor arena composed of high stone walls connecting to the back sides of private dwellings, Ganto laid his right forearm against Peter's chest to prevent his next step. "The cockpit is no place for a weak temperament," Ganto warned. "Before you enter, leave your sentiments behind."

"I'll be alright."

Halab slapped Peter on the back. "Sure he will, Ganto. We'll make an avid cocker out of him, you'll see."

Ganto carefully studied Peter's present disposition for reassurance.

"What are we waiting for?" Peter demanded.

Ganto nodded. "Right. You're right." He pushed open the gate and led the way into the cockpit.

The ground was perfectly level despite the onslaught of rain in the last two days. It was obvious that tremendous effort was taken to prepare this outdoor cockpit for today's set of matches.

There was a circular space of approximately ten cubits in diameter, which had been drained and pounded and covered lightly with straw. This acted as a foundation for the tightly woven mat that was rolled on top to serve as a stage floor. Along the rim of this matting ran a tightly woven length of fabric about a cubit high and tent-staked several paces apart in order to keep the gamecocks within the circular boundary set for their combat.

The arena was surrounded by numerous long benches placed intermittently, almost scattered haphazardly. But after closer examination of this seating, it became clear that this arrangement was sought to accommodate areas for a standing public's ability to mix with the seated for better viewing and wagering, as well as to provide an outlet for the nervous fluidity that was commonly produced upon the emotions of the men who were witnessing the cocks' mortal combat.

Although the majority of these games in Jerusalem were held surreptitiously, usually outside the city's walls, there were those who enjoyed Roman protection and flaunted Jewish Law. Judging by the appearance of its relative permanency, this outdoor arena seemed to possess this sort of sanction. And judging by the din of the audience, no effort was being made to conceal the approaching hour of this contest.

The atmosphere was tense with excitement and

anticipation. Pockets of heated debates and wager-making proliferated. A rough-looking character in one corner of the arena punctuated his vehemence against another with a blow to the man's head, which caused a minor riot in that section. Several officials ran to the scene and quickly suppressed the violent disorder.

Peter sensed the madness of the majority, its passions waiting to be fully unleashed by the sight of blood and mutilation and death.

The variety of men this place held was reflective of Jerusalem's cosmopolitan character. Greeks, Jews, Romans, Syrians, Egyptians—all and more were represented. Rich and poor, merchant and royal, mercenary and soldier, citizen and bandit—all stations were represented and all were held by their common lust for blood and gambling and drinking.

Peter redirected his attention to the cockpit for further study, but he was interrupted by an enthusiastically hard smack on the back by his new Syrian companion, Halab.

"What do you think!"

"It's . . . it's loud."

"You've heard nothing, yet." Halab rubbed the palms of his hands together with great relish. "Now, if you'll relinquish some of the contents of your purse, I'll be able to buy us a sack of wine *and* place a healthy wager or two for us."

Peter handed him the entire purse.

"What's this?" Halab's expression was mixed with surprise, delight, and horror.

"Take it."

"All? You trust me with it all?"

"I wasn't thinking of trust."

"It seems to me you're not thinking at all." Halab gawked at Ganto, hoping for clarification.

"He's strictly a Galilean," Ganto said. "But I'm, culturally, a Judean, as well."

Halab shrugged his shoulders. "So?"

"I don't know anything more about his kind than, oh, let's say, a Syrian like yourself would. Besides, like I've told you, he's a follower of that one who was crucified the day before yesterday. You know, the one they called Jesus of Nazareth."

"Ah. Yes, yes. Of course. I forgot." Halab's head turned violently in Peter's direction in a sudden display of recollection. "You know, I do remember something else about that lunatic, other than about his execution and—yes! Your king claimed to be related to *your* god, right?"

"I told you he *claimed* nothing," Peter said, intolerantly.

"Bah! No matter." Halab tapped Peter on the shoulder in a sincere expression of friendship. "Easy there. I respect all gods, remember? Even your storm god." Halab gulped down some wine. "Yahweh, Baal, whatever. The price is still a lamb, right Ganto? Ha!"

"But . . . but you still don't understand," Peter insisted. "Jesus was more than—"

"Yes, yes, yes, they all are," Halab placated. "It's alright. Believe me," he obliviously insisted. "I'm open to gods and prophets." Halab's face suddenly grew serious. "I'll not get angry with you again over this.

Like I said, I'm wide open." He leaned toward Peter. "Relax. A man *can* be too careful. Hell, in my last auxiliary cohort alone, we worshipped dozens of deities from as many cultures. Personally, even though a Syrian, I prescribed to the main gods of the legions. My official one, of course, was the Regimental Standard— our Eagle." Peter began to protest. "No, no, no. Listen to me first." Halab took a deep breath for dramatic effect. "I've seen many good results from the sacrifices at the camp's altar of the gods. Mars, of course, transcends them all among real soldiers and, for me, well, when I was a soldier, Mars had my allegiance. Then there was my personal favorite, Iuppiter Dolichenus, the god born where the iron is born." He noted Peter's resignation and Ganto's quizzical expression. "Oho, yes, Galilean and Judean. Still, both of you are Jews nonetheless."

"Bah!" Ganto retorted. "You know me, Halab. I believe only in myself. God, or gods, be damned. And don't accuse me of being a blood Judean. It's true, I've lived in this part of the land most of my life. But my roots are Galilean."

Halab shrugged his shoulders. "Fine. Whatever. It's no hair from my nostrils what you consider yourself, Ganto. Neither one way or the other does it matter to me. Hell, I've fought alongside men from all over the Empire who brought with them their own beliefs. You can't imagine the number of cults I've enjoyed the protection from, not only from my warrior brethren, but from local cults in places where I've been stationed. A man can't be too careful."

Ganto chuckled. "You're my best and most trusted man."

They grasped each other's right hand to express their comradeship.

"And you're a powerfully good bandit leader." Halab released his grip from Ganto's hand and turned to Peter. "You've grown quiet."

"I've grown more confused, that's all."

"About what?"

"My own beliefs. And about being careful."

"Get in line with the rest of us, right Ganto?"

"Right."

"Whenever I get confused," Halab pontificated, "I manage to find another minor local god, or goddess, to help me erase my concerns and bring me comfort. That was the one freedom the Roman army permitted—within reason, of course. But once you're stuck with one prophet—or worse!—with one god, well, then you're stuck with having to make too many justifications." Halab peered hard at Peter. "Is that your problem? One god? Of course. You're a Jew."

"But so am I," Ganto interjected. "And there's no confusion here."

Halab howled with laughter. "That's because you and I are alike. And beneath all this spiritual gibberish, you and I believe in ourselves first and foremost. What lies beneath my constant trading of deities and your lack of them at all is the profound assurance of ourselves." Halab lifted his eyebrows into a sly expression. "We believe in nothing but the sword and the flesh. Right, Ganto?"

"Right. And that translates into a good wager comforted by a sack of wine."

Halab shifted the purse of money from his right to his left hand as if he newly discovered it. "Right. Grab a bench for us if you can. I'll find you shortly." Then Halab reassured Peter. "Don't worry. More wine and a good match will subtract some of your woes. You'll see." Halab stepped toward the thickest area of the crowd and disappeared among the tumult.

"That's not a bad fellow," Peter said.

"I know. I've trusted him with my life on many occasions. Dependable and fearless, he is. But most of all, incredibly dependable. Let's find a bench."

Peter and Ganto weaved their way among the growing spectators looking for a permanent place near the pit. As they made their search, Ganto explained some of the cockpit's rules and regulations. "The birds have to be weighed-in first to prevent any unfair advantage. Then the judge records the birds' color markings and physical features to prevent any last moment switching of birds during a match. Cheating is famous among cockers. And they are generally poor sports over losing." He shrugged his shoulders philosophically. "Every game has its personality quirks among its players."

Ganto looked back at Peter and spotted an unoccupied long bench beside him, which Ganto had passed unnoticed while instructing his bewildered pupil. "Peter. There. Take that bench. Quick." Peter sidled in front of the open seating and declared it in his possession by his large and imposing presence. "Good one,

Peter. Sit down." Ganto sat beside him and continued with his instruction. "Now, the handlers have to abide by some rules, as well. First, when they bring their gamecocks into the pit, they have to display the birds so the judge and referee can verify their markings, proving them to be the birds designated for the match. Then, once the birds are set beak to beak on their starting lines and released, the handlers cannot touch them unless the birds get hung up into each other with their spurs or hung up in the matted floor or if they escape the pit or, heaven forbid, if they happen to quit fighting for thrice twenty counts. Under these circumstances, the handlers will take hold of their birds and quickly soothe their injuries before placing them on their starting lines again to continue their battle."

"What if the cocks continue to choose not to fight?" Peter asked.

"Ahh, yes, rare, generally speaking. And particularly rare at the beginning of a contest, but not unknown. It's more common after a lengthy battle when there's blood oozing from their mouths and their swollen tongues are protruding and they've been reduced to panting for air."

Peter's eyes widened. "I see."

"Oftentimes, the birds are simply dazed and shattered by the accumulation of wounds gained through the rigors of the battle. In such cases, it's up to the handlers to repair their birds and coax them into finishing the fight."

"But . . . but what if they don't?"

Ganto looked around cautiously and spoke softly

after leaning closely to Peter. "It's considered bad luck and bad form to talk of such matters at the pits. But there are rules for that possibility."

"And, they are?" Peter whispered.

"Well, if one cock refuses the battle, he's brought beak to beak with his opponent up to ten times or until he fights. If he doesn't, he loses the match."

"And both lives are saved?"

Ganto chuckled. "Not likely. The winner, of course, will live to see another contest. But the other's neck will be wrung by its owner for its cowardice."

"That's not fair!"

"The owner can do as he wills. Besides, what is fair?"

"I . . . simply meant that—"

"Never mind what you meant. You want to hear the remaining rules or not?" Peter kept silent so that Ganto could finish. "Now, if both cocks refuse to fight, a riot will break out in the arena." Ganto cackled loudly and nudged Peter's left upper arm with his right forearm. "That was a joke, my friend." Ganto's face flattened at Peter's lack of amusement. "Anyway, if both refuse to fight after ten placements on the pit's line, then another cock is brought into the match. Lots are cast between the two original handlers to see which of their cocks will fight the fresh one first. The loser places his game-cock against the new opponent and the winner takes up his cock and waits his turn in the pit." Ganto leaned against Peter and gestured with his hands for emphasis. "Now, if one fights the new opponent and the other doesn't, the fighter wins. If both refuse to fight or if both fight, then it is a drawn battle and both cocks will live to see another contest."

"What if one is killed by the fresh cock?"

"Well, if the other fights and survives, he wins. And, of course, if he fights and kills, he wins. But if he refuses, the dead cock who fought wins."

"And the one who refused to fight dies at the hands of his master."

"Naturally. Look! There's Halab. Halab! Over here."

Halab approached them, carrying a huge sack of wine. "I got the wine at a good price and, look, the barkeep even provided us with cups." Halab almost dropped the cups from his cradling arm. "Damn. Give me a hand here."

Ganto quickly came to his aid and snatched the cups from their precarious perch so Halab could set down the large wineskin that lay across his right shoulder. "We'll go blind before reaching the bottom of that skin."

Halab mischievously bared his large teeth. "Precisely." He carefully lowered the wineskin between him and Ganto. "The stakes over this coming battle are running high. Both cocks have fiery reputations. Proven warriors, both. Neither of them has been involved in a drawn match. Born and trained killers, both."

"And?"

"After this wine purchase and the cups—"

"I thought they were provided."

"With a deposit, of course."

"Thirty denarii. And I say we bet the lot of it." He and Ganto looked at Peter for his opinion.

"Do what you think best," Peter relinquished. "Both of you."

"Beautiful!" Halab shouted joyfully. "Then I'll stake the lot of it."

"That's fine with me," said Ganto.

The crowd was beginning to grow impatient, and many in the audience began to holler and stamp their feet and motion to the officials to start the game.

Halab wrenched the stopper from the wineskin and drank directly from it to assess its taste. "Not bad. A strong headache will follow, but not bad. Show me your cups." He filled Peter's cup to the brim, then the other two cups, which Ganto held.

As soon as Halab pressed the stopper into place, Ganto handed him a full cup.

"To your health."

All three clanked their cups together in a toast, then drank deeply. The cheap wine was remarkably pleasant and thick and fragrant.

The gamecocks were finally brought into the pit: one was already held in full display by its handler and the other was still concealed in its handler's linen bag. Peter was the first of them to notice. "Look at that! Are my eyes deceiving me? How long are his spurs?"

"Four fingers, it looks to me. Maybe five," said Halab, as he slithered past Ganto to Peter's other side to keep their cockfight virgin between them.

"So sharp. So lethal looking," Peter said with awe.

"Its keeper makes sure of its point by scraping the spur with a sharp knife."

"I see." Peter studied the bird.

"You act as if you've never seen a cock," said Ganto.

For Peter, the sight and sound of any cock rekindled his shame and torment. "Almost always in full plumage," he answered without expression.

"What's that? What did you say?"

"I've always seen them in their natural feathered dress," Peter shouted.

"I see. But you have seen them young."

"Of course."

"And bred."

"Sure. Even some in early training."

"But this is your first view of the pits," Halab stated emphatically for confirmation.

"Of course."

"Don't sound so superior."

"Was I? I . . . I'm sorry."

"Don't be. You're about to lose your sup—your, virginity. Right, Ganto?"

Halab and Ganto laughed as if they were sharing some kind of ridiculous conspiracy.

"Naked-heeled," Ganto added. "That gamecock is naked-heeled. That means a long and fierce combat to the death, Peter."

"Especially if the one still in the bag matches this blue-breasted cock's size and strength and heel," said Halab. "If so, I wager that their fight will go as long as two hours."

"I'll not wager against that. But I'd almost lay silver on that blue-breasted one that's on display without seeing the other still in his handler's linen bag."

Halab nudged Peter. "What do you think?"

Peter drank some wine and shrugged. "Don't know one from the other. My bet would be a guess."

"And as good a guess as anybody else's."

"Come on, then." Halab insisted with good-natured sincerity. "Look at them. Study them. Give us your best guess."

"But . . . but why?"

Halab showed him the thirty denarii purse. "I'm wagering on beginner's luck. The virgin's eye. The oracle of ignorance. Come on, my man. Humor me. Study the birds. Then pick one."

Peter peered through the tumult of the spectators into the pit where the fowl keepers and handlers, referees and judges were preparing to weigh in and inspect the first feather-armored warrior on display. He tried to concentrate through the din of wager making, arguments over seating, demands for drink, and numerous surreptitious activities that Peter was unable to decipher even though he was certain that it was all connected to the high stakes of the forthcoming battle. He saw money changing hands and mortally serious glances exchanged. Peter redirected his attention to where the cocks were being staged for battle.

The officials were inspecting the blue-breasted cock's markings, while its awaiting opponent clucked and chuckled from inside a large linen bag.

Peter shifted uneasily on his bench. He felt the burning eyes of his companions, drank some wine, and concentrated on the bird. The cock was placed on the weighing scale's sling.

He was aghast at how severe the gamecock had been trimmed of its plumage. Its original magnificence had been sheared and cut and plucked from him. In his opinion, the cock had already been mutilated before ever stepping into the forthcoming carnage of the pit.

"So, what do you think?" Halab eagerly demanded. "That one's a killer, don't you think?"

Peter nervously glanced at him.

"Give him the time he needs," Ganto retorted, as he slapped Halab on the back with the flat of his hand. "Let the man think!"

The gamecock weighed in at five litras. The handler took him off the weighing sling and presented him to another judge for further inspection.

The bird possessed a red back and a yellow-green tail. He was a stocky, dark blue-breasted fowl, trimmed of all his naturalness in the following manner: First, and most obviously, the fowl's wattle, the red fleshy pendant that hung below the beak, was surgically cut from him—along with his comb. Secondly, the cock's hackle was trimmed down to a narrow mane from the root of the comb, along the back of the head, down the long neck to the ridge between his shoulders. Thirdly, his tail and wings were cut short and the feathers from below his rump to his belly had been plucked, as well as the feathers from around the head, neck, and tail. And lastly, the little warrior's upper beak had been sharpened to a point and its lower beak had been filed shorter. Peter imagined that this had been done to improve his mouth's hold when seizing its opponent.

"What do you think?" Halab breathed impatiently.

"Give me a minute, damn it! The other cock hasn't been let out of the bag, yet!"

"He's right, Halab. Drink your wine and leave him alone."

"Alright, alright."

Peter admired the strength of the thick muscular thighs but was still amazed at the length of the spurs, which were thick at the ankle, tapered along the shank, and sharpened into deadly points. The spurs were as indestructible looking as the strongest and hardest briar he'd ever seen.

Ganto leaned closer to Peter and spoke to him with an instructing tone in an attempt to placate Halab's impatience. "As I told you earlier, those naked heels will insure a long battle. They are weapons provided by nature that can and will inflict mortal damage, to be sure. That one shows real signs of courage. See the pride of his bearing? See the way he turns his head and cranes his powerful long neck? And his eyes, just look how they lust for a kill."

"That fowl has a high bearing," Halab interjected. "That's favorable."

"He's right."

"And I'll wager he's sharp-heeled."

"I can see that for myself," Peter said.

Ganto suppressed his amusement. "What Halab means—well, just look." The handler placed the game-cock on the ground. The cock treaded the pit with tremendous loftiness, its gait narrow and sure. "See? I agree with Halab. He appears sharp-heeled." Again, he perceived Peter's lack of understanding. "That means every time that blue-breasted cock flaps his modified wings in order to rise for a hit, he will draw blood from his opponent with his spurs."

"I see."

The cock crowed frequently, piercing Peter's consciousness to the bone. He wanted to cry out to his Master, suddenly, but Ganto enthusiastically grabbed him by the back of his neck. "The power of that cock sends a chill through me as well. What do you think, Halab?"

"He possesses true courage, I think. And wit, yes, a smart bird he seems to be." Halab's eyes were strongly focused on the cock. "I predict he rises well in combat." He leaned against Peter for emphasis as he spoke to Ganto, who ardently leaned against Peter on the other side. "I really do believe he's carrying a set of bloody heels." Halab pressed his face closer to his virgin companion's face.

Peter responded to the man's wine-soaked breath, as well as to the general confinement of his two pressing cohorts. "Come on, you two." He pushed both of them away with his forearms. "Give me some space. I need space to think. I need to study the other cock."

"Yes, yes, of course, of course," Halab agreed as he turned his own attention to a linen bag held by the other handler. "Yes. The weigh-in for the other bird is forthcoming. Look!"

The handler carefully untied the large linen bag and allowed his cock to arise from it. The gamecock's head and neck appeared first like a dangerous serpent looking for something to strike; its eyes inscrutable, its viperlike movement terrifying. The spectators came to a momentary hush, in awe of the majestic creature. And when the handler dramatically released the open end of the linen bag, it dropped to the ground like a curtain to reveal a gallant bird. The crowd cheered and resumed wagering with increased zeal.

"By the gods!" Halab whooped. "Killers, both—magnificent!"

"They're gladiators, to be sure!" Ganto concurred.

The second bird sported a black breast and tail. Its back and shoulders were silver white. His face was brilliantly red with red dilated eyes that sparkled with intensity.

"His eyes are like rubies!"

"Yes. And look at his beak."

"Eagle-like."

"And the rest of him, clipped and trimmed to perfection."

"He looks like a hunter."

"They both do! The other one is equally menacing. Look!"

The handler picked up his black-breasted cock for weighing.

"What do you think, now?" Halab declared, insisting on an answer from Peter.

"I . . . I'm not sure. Both of them seem formidable."

"Look again. They only appear equally matched. One of them has a weakness that is not presently plain to the eye. And one of them is going to die because of that weakness. Look at them. Go on. Study them hard. Thirty denarii will be wagered on one of them. Which one will it be?"

Ganto frowned at Halab to desist from further pressure against their companion.

The black-breasted cock was weighed in at five and a quarter litras. The quarter litra difference intensified the chatter among those gathered around the pit. The cock was lifted from the weighing sling and, after a judge inspected the bird's markings, the handler set him on the ground to tread freely. At the same time, the other handler picked up the blue-breasted cock to prevent a premature engagement of the two birds.

The handsome black-breasted cock clucked and crowed defiantly as he strutted about the pit displaying his compact and sinewy body. His natural spurs were equal to his blue-breasted opponent's. Suddenly, the bird spread his trimmed wings to express a savagery so primal that Peter stood up in response. The other two stood up to catch what Peter saw.

"What!" Halab demanded.

"Something dangerous."

"Yes?"

"Within that bird lies something dangerous." Peter trembled in the wake of his declaration to prevent himself from verbally revealing the suicidal regret lurking within him.

"Hear that, Ganto? That's good enough for me."

"I'm with you," said Ganto. "The beginner's eye is often the best."

"That black-breasted gladiator is the one for us." Halab dashed away from them toward a small huddle of men to make his thirty denarii wager.

Peter managed to regain some internal composure.

"I . . . I hope I'm not leading you two in the wrong direction." He drank the rest of his wine to further steady himself.

Ganto guzzled the rest of his wine. "It's your purse. And it's all a gamble." He took Peter's empty cup from him and stooped over the wineskin to refill his cup. "Besides, it doesn't matter. Anything can happen in a cockfight." He handed Peter a full cup and refilled his own. "And as strong as those two warriors are, we'll be dead drunk before one is mortally wounded." He stoppered the wineskin, stood up, and leaned toward Peter. "Drink. Cheers. Be merry."

"Yes. Be merry." Peter stared at the birds and the officials in the cockpit. The din of the crowd was almost a relief from his own loud thoughts over his Master and his own triple denial of him. One of the cocks crowed and forced him to press his free hand against his left ear to keep himself from going mad.

Ganto tugged the back of Peter's tunic. "Are you alright?"

Peter lowered his hand and simply nodded, yes. Then he focused his attention at the pit as Ganto encouraged him to sit down.

Both combatants showed no inclination to fight when the second handler decided to release his bird into the freedom of the pit. The spectators were displeased with their dance about the pit and they threw impatient invectives at the handlers as the cocks stood and glared at each other for an excessive period of time.

Halab, having returned from making his wager, nudged Peter with his elbow. "Don't worry. These are the favored cocks in today's set of matches. They'll fight well."

Peter blinked his eyes in dismay. He wanted to tell Halab that he wasn't worried. He wanted to tell him that he wasn't supposed to be here. Then he turned to the cockpit to face the horror of this impending small death.

Halab nudged him again. "I still believe you're right. The black-breasted one: he's the more courageous fighter. Right?" He looked at Peter for some kind of reassurance, but Peter's facial expression was flat. "Well, anyway, our money has been placed on him."

"And how will they judge who's the winner?" Peter's tone was equally flat and matched the blankness of his eyes.

Halab peered at Peter as if he were insane. "As in any battle to the death, the cock who's left standing on his feet is the victor."

"And the other?" Peter said unwittingly.

Halab peered at him with continued astonishment. "Surely the wine hasn't got to your head already! *The other*? The other is dead, of course."

Peter felt Ganto's heavy gaze. "What?"

"I told you the rules."

"I wanted to hear it from another source. I wanted to hear it again."

Ganto shook his head. "You're peculiar."

"Humor me, the virgin with the thirty denarii wager, alright?"

Peter turned to Halab. "So, then, to be left standing isn't the only criterion?"

Halab seemed relieved. "Oh, I see. Yes, yes. Good question. Well, in fact, standing is no criterion at all, really. Only life. And death. And life, of course, wins. So, if neither is standing, it's in the breath. Victory is in the continued breath of the winner's life. See?" Halab looked into the pit. "Don't worry. Those two in there are great handlers. Their cocks will soon engage in their mortal combat. Don't worry. You'll see."

Peter wasn't worried. And he didn't want to see! But he saw the blood lust in the eyes of many spectators.

Halab noted the change in Peter's expression. "I said, don't worry."

"I'm not!"

"And just wait," Halab continued, oblivious to Peter's irritability. "Like Ganto told you, naked-heeled fighting is grand. It makes for long combat. Two, even three hours long—potentially. And with that length of time in the pits, you can admire the character of the birds: their strength, courage, stamina, wit—everything that has to do with life. And death." Halab spilled some wine from his cup as he leaned enthusiastically against Peter. "One of those cocks is going to die, by the gods. Maybe both! But in dying well, they live!"

Peter was choking from the strain. "What . . . what do they feed them?"

"Ahh! That's a secret among professional trainers," Halab answered fervently.

"Really?"

"Bread steeped in urine, for one," Ganto interjected.

"Ridiculous," Peter said.

"Not to these people," Halab said in Ganto's defense. "They will quarrel with a post concerning the proper care of these crazy birds. Right, Ganto?"

"Absolutely."

The pit was cleared of everybody except the two handlers, a referee, and the two gamecocks. The betting continued vociferously. The handlers held their birds and displayed them to the other in order to taunt the cocks into anger.

"What are they doing?"

"Encouraging them to fight."

The birds began to strike at each other from a distance.

"Place them on their marks!" Halab shouted. "Place them on their marks, you bastards!"

There was a long amber line of parched grain at the center of the pit and two short amber lines drawn almost a cubit away from the center mark on either side, which served as the starting points for each cock.

"Set them on their marks, damn you!" Halab shouted.

To their marks they were set, to everybody's delight, followed by the judge's call to "release!"

The fierce black-breasted cock charged and caught hold of the blue-breasted cock's trimmed hackle by his sharpened beak, leaped and flapped into the air, and struck his opponent several times in the chest with his sharp spurs. A little higher and it would have been to the throat and, therefore, could have been mortal. As it was, blood oozed through the feathers, which was unnoticed by the stricken warrior who managed to disengage himself from his attacker. The injured cock quickly retaliated with a leap and a double strike at the black-breasted cock's head, which successfully blinded his adversary's left eye by the gouge of his pointed, and now bloody, spur.

"Damn!" Halab shouted. "Look at those two warriors! Who could have doubted them for a moment? And look, already with bloody heels!" He directed himself at Peter. "When I was stationed at Caesarea Palaestinae, I was able to go to the Great Amphitheatre of Herod's and enjoy the circus. I swear to you that the gladiators I witnessed, who struggled for their lives with swords and spears, did not face their game of death as bravely as these two gamecocks already have in this pit. Look at them. By the gods. Our black-breasted beauty fights as well with one eye as he would have with two!"

The area surrounding the pit was a human scene of pandemonium, confusion, and disorder. And after the handlers regained control of their disengaged gamecocks, there was a noticeable increase of shouting over additional or changed wagers. Men jostled each other for better viewing positions as they waited for the handlers to reposition their cocks at their parched grain marks. Both combatants were already hurt, one partially blinded, the other wounded at the breast, and both already covered in blood and dust. Excitement increased despite the lull in combat as the handlers quickly doctored their birds: sucking blood from their wounds, wiping blood from their heads, spitting chewed herbs for healing onto either an injured eye or directly into a raw eye socket—all quickly done in preparation for the second round of their battle.

When ready, the chickens were placed on their marks and the handlers waited for the judge to call for their release. The judge delayed the call and calculated the increased tumult-giving pleasure of the onlookers until the spectacle had reached what he considered to be a climax.

Halab jostled Peter into irritability. "What do you think of the pits so far, my new friend? Come on, tell me."

"I . . . I don't know."

"You hear that, Ganto?"

Peter turned to him, interested to hear what a kinsman had to say about this blood sport. "You hear that?"

Ganto smirked. "Bringing the cockfights to Palestine is the only good thing Rome has done for us. I've earned quite a few denarii from the pits."

"Gambling is generally not to my liking," Peter countered.

"You've generally not the stomach for blood, you mean."

"I didn't say that," Peter said guardedly. "But our laws, our laws disapprove of gambling."

"Our laws are impotent. It's Rome and Herod who rule. And they are as corrupt as everyone in here." Ganto noticed the shock in Peter's face. "Yes. I include you." Ganto grinned. "For a man your size, your mouth twitches too much. You've a heart of a woman, I think."

Peter's eyes hardened from the insult. "Watch it, Ganto. I don't take well to bullying—from anybody."

"Then that makes you a better man than Judas?"

"And your dealings with him. What were they?"

Ganto's grin turned into a smirk. "You really don't know? What kind of delusion is this? Judas's relations with me and my band was no secret. Your Master encouraged it."

"Say, what's this?" Halab interjected. "I thought we settled that sort of thing earlier?"

"Not now, Halab," Ganto cautioned.

Halab stiffened in response to Ganto's hardened attitude, but let the moment between them pass without confrontation. Halab turned his attention back to the cockpit to study the birds and drink his wine.

"As I said," Ganto continued over the din of the crowd, "your Master encouraged it."

"That's not true," said Peter.

"Then your Master kept you in the dark—where you remain."

"Isn't his Master dead?" Halab demanded.

"Damn it, Halab, stay out of this!"

"Alright, alright, I'm out," he said, feigning hurt feelings before returning his gaze to the pit.

"Then enlighten me," Peter demanded.

"For what? He's dead and gone."

"Yes. Like Judas."

This glimmer of news caught Ganto's interest. "What do you know about Judas? What have they done to him?"

"It's what he's done to himself," Peter said. "He hanged himself."

Halab quietly shifted his attention back to his intense companions.

Ganto's face became animated with a mixture of surprise and amusement. "Well, I'll be damned. He had a little pluck in him after all."

"It wasn't courage that gave him strength to do it."

"How would you know? A man's mettle comes in many forms. Sometimes it surfaces at the oddest times. In his case, at the hour of death. Good one, Judas! At least in death you were a man!"

"He didn't look like one when I saw him hanging from that rafter."

"Because the man was already gone, you idiot. You took him down, I hope."

"We did."

"And?"

"We buried him among some trees."

"You and your—his—brethren."

"That's right."

Ganto nodded his head. "And so be it."

"Release!"

The crowd exploded with an ecstatic roar in response to the judge's command. All three men turned toward the fury of the pits.

The cocks hurled themselves at each other with a startling ferocity. The blue-breasted cock leaped and fluttered like a flame and struck the black-breasted cock squarely in the chest. The hit was dreadfully powerful and the bird staggered backward like a drunkard. The blue breast charged relentlessly to issue a finishing stroke that missed and caused him to totter momentarily onto its own breast. The black-breasted cock managed to right itself off his rump and circle around to his opponent's left where he grabbed the upper portion of the blue breast's right wing with his beak and struck him numerous times with his damaging spurs. He managed to slash and tear at the blue-breasted warrior's abdomen before he lost hold of his opponent's wing. The gutted blue-breasted cock responded to his monstrous and painfully bloody condition with a squawk of anguish.

Passions rose high among the bird watchers: cheers and jeers thundered all around as the audience enjoyed the horror of the scene.

"In ancient Syria," Halab shouted to Peter, "I heard there were many who worshipped the fighting cock. Worshipped, I say!" The crowd roared. "Look at those two warriors fight! Is there anything more beautiful?"

The shattered black breast rallied with a counterattack and seized his foe by the hackle. Together, they leaped into the air and thumped onto the pit's floor where they tumbled like a ball of feathers and claws and crows inseparable to the audience's eye and ear. When their rolling came to a stop, the handlers were quick to approach their birds in order to separate them, since all four spurs were embedded into flesh.

Blood oozed through the feathers of the dusty birds. Part of one claw was broken at the apex of the black-breasted cock's heel, and blood covered the eyes of the blue-breasted cock from a wound that dripped from the bird's head.

The relative lull in the gathering was caused by the delay required to shift their unruliness from the maimed and mangled cocks to the many betting disputes concerning the development of the battle. Blows were exchanged among the spectators over this unholy game, which aroused further savagery among them.

The handlers managed to skillfully remove the impaled spurs from their cocks and separate the entangled birds who continued to claw and nip at each other. Then, the handlers scurried to opposite sides of the pit with their battered and enfeebled creatures. Blood flowed freely from their birds' wounds, and the handlers quickly began to apply their healing arts in preparation for the next round of battle.

Peter was infected by this cruel and brutal amusement. He was horrified with himself and, yet, drawn to its savagery. He heard both cocks crow and pant and clap their wings to express their pain. "It's just like life, isn't it? Quick and mean and deadly. Without good cause. Without meaning other than the moment." Peter drained his cup of wine and allowed Halab to refill it as Ganto spoke exuberantly.

"That's right. You've got it now."

"He's a quick study," Halab added.

"And how else can the poor and homeless have a good time?"

"Not to mention the thieves and the pickpockets," said Halab.

Ganto joined him in laughter. "But seriously, Peter, at a cockfight, everybody forgets their differences."

"Right," Halab chimed. "Drink up!"

And Peter drank.

"A low-life Syrian deserter from a Roman auxiliary legion can stand elbow to elbow—"

"With a scoundrel bandit that might end up cruci-fied with him one day."

Peter studied Ganto and the Syrian during their strange banter that sounded like humor by their laugh-ter, but seemed to convey something darker between them. He interrupted them before this unexpected seri-ousness grew any further. "Why do the handlers remove the gamecock's comb and wattles?"

"It's an important step in its development, you know, to prepare a cock for battle," Halab answered. He noticed Peter's confused expression. "It renders them less likely to injury during a conflict against another bird. It'd be torn from its lower beak anyway."

"And the clipped wings?"

"To keep them cooler—"

"And to prevent them from flying out of the pit—"

"And it's less of something for his opponent to get a hold of with his beak. Once pinned, the spurs will fly. Understand?"

Peter simply nodded and gazed into the pit to watch the handlers care for their birds. They were a grizzly pair of characters who wore rags for tunics. One appeared to be on the verge of leprosy, and the other looked to be seriously alcoholic. In either case, they seemed to handle their gamecocks with great skill and delicacy.

One of the handlers spit on the bird's head and rubbed the spittle into its crown. The other was licking his bird's neck as if his tongue were a diagnostic instru-ment testing the condition of the bird's wounds.

The madness of this assembly could be felt and seen

as well as heard. The spectators continued to lay wagers and issue blows at one another with an alarming frequency. Despite the din, chuckles of defiance could be heard from the bruised and battered birds. They looked fiercer than ever despite their raw injuries. Both were writhing their necks like serpents and struggling to break their handler's hold to kill their opponents.

"Pit them!" Peter heard the judge command. He could not fail to admire the incredible courage and stamina displayed by these cocks.

The sound of thunder declared the unusual weather's presence. Peter looked up into a dark bank of clouds and, from the corner of his eyes, saw a quiver of lightning reveal itself like a hairline crack on a pot under a good light, then vanish soundlessly into the gray sky. Rain began to fall in large drops. But nobody took notice. Shoulders hunched over, hands served as lids over cups, flat palms became visors over eyes.

Peter was too drunk to feel discomfort. He drained his cup and allowed it to be refilled again.

"Pit them!" the judge yelled once again.

The crowd's cheer intensified. Halab's and Ganto's eyes were anchored to the game.

"Those are not an ordinary pair of roosters!" Halab shouted to Ganto.

"There's no pleasure more exciting than the pleasure of cocking!" said Ganto in response.

The handlers set the cocks on the redrawn grain line and, once again, the judge delayed the start until the diabolical drama of the surrounding spectacle reached the maximum height of its cold-blooded barbarity.

"Release!"

The cocks hurled themselves into battle. They sprang into the air and, for a short while, they were mortally locked in a chaotic ball of wings and feathers and legs. They tumbled apart, rallied, and attacked each other with ghastly determination. The blue-breasted cock managed to bury the sharp point of its angry beak into the already blinded eye of the other while anchored to his opponent's body by its spurs. He pecked and gouged as if digging for a pearl until he managed to reveal his opponent's bloody socket. Despite the torture issued by his adversary, the black-breasted cock managed to spur his opponent numerous times—but, most significantly, his last blow hit the blue-breasted cock in the neck, causing a cry of agony so profound that there were many in the stands who sucked in their breaths in response. Again, they tumbled and rolled over and over on top of each other, kicking up dust from the mat, hitting and bouncing off one of the rim stakes, then rolling into an exhausted heap. They were hung up together by their spurs; only three were buried deeply, this time. The black-breasted cock's left leg was broken and projecting hideously in the wrong anatomical direction.

The handlers reached for their weary gamecocks and cruelly ripped them from each other in an attempt to enlarge the wounds of their opponents. Then they quickly smoothed their birds' ruffled plumage and retreated to the opposite sides of the pit, leaving a crimson puddle of blood on the floor where the birds had come to a stop.

The carnage began to make Peter feel sick. He stood up and swayed unsteadily. "I've got to leave." He tried to get by Halab.

"Where are you going? There's plenty of wine, don't worry." Halab pulled Peter back onto the bench with a heavy hand to the shoulder. "Drink up. This match will be legendary!"

The rain ceased as quickly as it had started. It succeeded in soaking everybody into a meaner and more uncomfortable state.

Peter watched the tender incongruity of the handlers' nursing care. Great pains were being taken to prolong their cocks' combat.

Both cocks were bleeding from multiple puncture wounds, gouged eyes, broken and torn limbs, and slashed abdomens. They were horribly crippled and exhausted and sweating profusely and, yet, their savage natures persisted: each bird trembled with the desire to conquer or die.

Peter sat feeling numb and wet and drunk. He heard the cheers and the start of another round, but he couldn't bring himself to look. He drank and he listened as he lamented his cruel fate, his depraved state; he drank himself toward an oblivion that took well over an hour to achieve.

The end finally, and mercifully, came when the blue-breasted cock managed to seize the other's mane, in a lucky moment of desperation, before issuing two fatal blows: one to the head and one to the heart. The black-breasted cock's shrill death crow was followed by a cruel applause. Peter peered at the gory sight and flinched. He saw the blue-breasted victor flap his defiant wings and crow over his dead opponent, then the triumphant cock staggered sideways and died.

Without hesitation, the winning spectators cheered as they turned to the losers and stakeholders to demand their money.

"We lost," Peter murmured. Then he noticed the dumbfounded expression on Halab's face.

"Easy come, easy go," Peter heard Ganto say.

This was the last thing Peter clearly remembered. There were more cock matches and a steady flow of wine until twilight, then two kinds of darkness descended upon Peter after the three of them stumbled out of the arena into separate directions: one from the sky and the other from the mind. Both led him toward the unconsciousness he sought and the abandonment he felt he deserved.

Peter staggered into the Jerusalem night blinded by his drunkenness. And when he reached a dead end in a dark alley, he simply lay his hurt body on the muddy ground and passed out.

Chapter 4

The Resurrection

Darkness enveloped the figure that stood before him and, yet, Peter felt the need to shade his eyes with the edge of his left palm pressed against his brow. He squinted at the translucent figure, trying to make it more than a shadow. "Who are you?"

"You know me," the figure said. "Otherwise you'd be afraid."

Peter burst into an uncontrollable laughter. "How . . . how," he wheezed, "how would I know when I wasn't afraid? Unafraid. Afraid. Unafraid. Afraid. Where's the separation? Where's—. Master. Is it you? Please. Is that you?" The shadow began to dissolve. "No. Wait. Don't go. Please. Whoever you are, please, answer one question."

The shadow's figure became more distinct again. It seemed to wait. "Is . . . is atonement for past sins truly possible? I was wrong. I've done wrong to leave my Master!"

"There is atonement. But the pain of guilt must always remain within you as long as you are alive."

"Then what is the point of God's forgiveness?"

"To prevent this guilt from becoming unbearable."

"Is that all?"

"Shouldn't that be enough?"

"But the pain, *the pain*." Peter persisted with tremendous anguish. "The pain—"

"Will go away at the time of death." The dark figure presented its hands to display the ragged puncture wounds above them at the wrists. "You see?"

Peter extended his right arm and managed to touch one of the wounds. His forefinger sank into the cavity where the cold sent a chill through him and forced him to recoil his arm. "That's no comfort!"

"Then one must suffer until kissed by the face of God."

"The face of God. Yes. The face of God will end my suffering. Will you kiss me?"

The figure began to laugh as it dissolved into the surrounding darkness.

"No! Wait!" Peter insisted.

But the darkness persisted to grow until it dissolved the figure and enveloped what was light and dark and pushed what was left of Peter's thoughts into another dream that would not be recollected until he was disturbed by the reality of the outside world—bringing him back to the actual presence of himself.

214

Peter twitched, in response to the tap tap tap of the heavy drops of rain. He raised his head from his wrecked body and squinted into the early morning light of sunrise. His eyes hurt. The orange disc near the horizon taunted him through this odd rain that came down in huge, sparse drops.

He was curled up in a ball and lying on his side with his back against an alley wall. He didn't know how he got there. He didn't know anything except that his face was swollen and he was soaked to the bone and he was going to be alright because . . . because: the distant memory of his receded vision was coming back into view again, despite the aching pain that racked his body. His joints cracked as he straightened his body and sat up. "I'm forgiven. Jesus! He's forgiven me, I know it."

"Peter? Peter. Is that you?"

Peter squinted at two approaching figures. He rubbed his eyes with his hands in an effort to uncloud his sight. They were not shadows.

"Peter, it's me."

"John? Is that you?"

Both men crouched beside Peter.

"Where have you been? We've been looking all over for you," said John.

"I . . . I was at—"

"My place for a time."

Peter surveyed the unfamiliar man. "Your place?"

"I'm Aaron. You helped fix my wall, remember?"

"Ah. Yes. Your wall, yes."

"You left his dwelling before we had a chance to make our way back. We just missed you."

"You missed me by far more than that," said Peter. "Where have you been?"

"Looking for you," John said plaintively. "And everybody else. Scattered. We're all so scattered."

Peter licked his lips. "I saw him, John."

Aaron and John exchanged a furtive glance.

"Saw? Saw who?" John coaxed.

"Our Master. He's alive. I swear. I saw him."

"Are . . . are you sure?" John inquired steadily.

"Don't look at me like I'm crazy."

"I'm not. I assure you. I . . . I . . . you tell him, Aaron."

Peter turned his imploring gaze to Aaron, who shifted his weight onto his knees.

"Tell me what?"

"Thaddaeus saw him as well," Aaron said.

"From a distance," John qualified.

"Just as he was awakening," Aaron further stipulated. "But saw him nonetheless."

"But that's not all," John added.

"What?"

"There were others—"

"Who saw him?" Peter interrupted.

"Yes." John peered at Aaron for support.

"Well?" Peter anxiously pressed his back against the alley wall. "Who?"

"It . . . it was Mary of Magdala and . . . and your own mother who saw that our Lord had risen."

"At his tomb? My . . . my own mother as well?"

"So it seems," said John.

"And at the foot of his cross. They were—" Peter

216

rubbed his dry, cracked lips with the back of his hand. "My mother is certainly not one for idle tales."

"And neither is Mary."

Peter's face twitched. "Yes. No. But why—I mean—they, our women, of all people, have seen him when . . . when. . . . " Peter suppressed the disconcerted tone in his voice and remained quietly harassed for a long time. "My view of him was not from a distance," he said emphatically. His eyes shifted guardedly from John to Aaron and back. "I touched him." Their response was not sufficient to dispel his insecurity. "I touched him, I said!" Peter crossed his arms against his chest and rocked himself from side to side. "Women," he muttered. Peter became still, his eyes betrayed his jealousy. "The two of you are not toying with me, are you?" His eyes darkened. "If you're toying with me, I swear—"

"I wouldn't do that," said John. "You should know by now that my humor is not of that kind."

Peter leaned forward, resting his forearm against the thighs of his crossed legs. He was emotionally exhausted.

John and Aaron remained silent as Peter released a long sigh followed by a long convulsive sob. When he finally lifted his eyes to them, they were shining. "He's risen from the dead. He's returned, like he said he would. And *I* saw him. *I* felt the cold wound to one of his wrists. I . . . *I*."

John peered at Aaron uneasily before he sat beside Peter. "Tell us more about what happened?"

Peter shrugged his shoulders. "He appeared twice. I touched him once. We spoke both times."

"Of what?"

Peter squirmed uneasily, then pressed his back against the wall. "He asked me, *'Did I love him more than these?'* "

"These what?"

Embarrassed, Peter answered, "I don't know. I was too overjoyed to ask and too afraid to break the spell of my second vision. I was so grateful to hear his—"

"Yes, yes, our Master hasn't changed his manner. But what did you say?"

"Yes," Aaron inserted. "Did you answer him?"

"Of course!"

"And!"

"I said, *'You know that I love you.'* "

"Good." Aaron nodded. "Good answer."

John gazed at Aaron and pressed his right forefinger against his lips in a gesture for silence. "Peter. Continue."

Peter searched his memory. "Well, I . . . I don't want to sound self-serving."

"It's too late for that now," said John. "I don't care about any of that. Just tell me what the two of you said."

Peter took a deep breath. " *'Take care of my lambs,'* he said. Then, then he called me Simon for the second time. *'Simon, son of John.'* "

"And why not Peter?" John queried with intense curiosity.

"I . . . I don't know. I wanted to ask him but . . . but—"

"What?"

"He . . . he asked me if I loved him, again. So, my thoughts naturally turned away from myself."

"And?"

"I said, *'Yes, Lord, you know that I love you.'* Then he said, *'Take care of my sheep.'* And harassed me a third time with the same question."

"The exact same?"

"Yes: *'Simon, son of John, do you love me?'* " Peter was disturbed and sad and bewildered. He searched John's and Aaron's eyes. "I'm nothing, I know that now."

"Yes, yes, but what did you say?"

"What else could I say but, *'Lord, you know everything; you know that I love you!'* "

John shook his head. "Peter, Peter, will you never stop yelling at him?"

"No. No! You don't understand. I was shouting, yes. But at myself. Myself! Because . . . because. . . ."

"Don't stop there," Aaron prodded.

"Because I believe he's forgiven me for my denials."

"Ah," John said with understanding. "Mara told us about your denials."

"Yes. Mara." Peter nodded his head bitterly. "She left me." He noticed their confusion. "No matter. That's another matter." He became irritated by their persistent confusion. "She doesn't matter!" He drew a deep breath. "Never mind. Yes. There were three denials before the cock crowed: as he predicted. Three denials. Followed by three tests and three charges."

"From your vision," Aaron qualified.

"*No.* Not a vision. No." His eyes blazed with

confirmation. "*He was real.* I know it." Peter sat up more confidently. "His three questions about my love were his sign of forgiveness, don't you see? He not only forgave me for each of my denials, he told me to follow him, to take care of his lambs." He wiped his nose with the back of his forearm. "And I will, I swear. I'll follow him to the bitter end, I swear, I'll—"

"Easy, Peter," said John as he pressed a calm hand upon Peter's shoulder.

"But . . . but what is our mission without his guidance?" Aaron asked cautiously. He threw a puzzled glance at John. "Where is his kingdom? What do we do now?"

"We're going to sit steadily and wait," John answered with great determination. "Another sign will come. More of his message will reach us." The tone in his voice was too fervent. "I know it. I know it!"

"Patience," Aaron uttered carefully. "He will come again—I hope."

Peter stirred restlessly. "I may have been forgiven—even invited, again, to follow him. But I . . . I don't know enough, feel worthy enough to be an apostle. For God's sake just . . . just look at us. We're a shabby lot. That's right: worn and threadbare, petty and mean."

"Don't speak that way," John pleaded.

"Sure, sure, easy for you to say. He loved you best."

"He loved us all!"

"But you. Always you he confided with—"

"And Judas and you—"

"He always challenged! Not confided. Me? Bah!"

John grimaced after licking the acidity from his lips. "You were almost second in command."

"Almost," Peter said resentfully.

"That's right. If you'd been smart enough to lead."

"Easy, John," cautioned Aaron. "I don't understand what this is about between you. But, well, look at him. He's still not recovered from his drunken fever." To Peter: "Don't take John seriously."

"I'm recovered. This leftover reek of wine you smell is not affecting me. I'm recovered!" The other two held their breaths. "But to what? To this pitiful congregation of frightened and confused idiots?"

"You seem to have placed yourself on a lofty level of judgment."

"Oh no, John. I'm describing myself, as well. In fact, I'm the lead idiot—no longer almost second in command." Peter gestured at his general condition. "See? Look at my depraved appearance. What kind of fool do I look like?"

"A frightened one," Aaron said. "You're right. And a confused one, like the rest of us idiots." His clownish method of delivery brought a smile to John's and Peter's faces; a cascade of verbal eagerness followed:

"We are lost—"

"And yet, we are bound."

"To become—"

"His apostles—"

"Of course!"

"And bound—"

"To him, even after death—"

"Which no longer exists—"

"Because of his death?"

"No. Because of his life. His resurrection. He was

flesh, I tell you. He was flesh! I touched him. And I know."

"Then what shall we do next?"

"Wait. That's what we're bound to do."

"Because that's all there's left to do."

"Is this part of the faith, my brothers?"

"No. No. It's all of it." Peter leapt to his feet with excitement. "And he's bound to show himself to me, again."

"You think so?"

Without notice or invitation, Peter started walking toward the nearby crowded street of the city. It had stopped raining.

"Where are you going?" John asked.

"To offer my humble prayers at the tomb of his resurrection."

"Yes! Good. But . . . but then what?"

"Then . . . then it's time to go back to fishing."

John stroked his bright red beard in dismay. "We haven't cast our nets in years."

"We have to eat," said Peter. "So, I'll cast my nets until . . . until, well, until I hear his next call."

"Ah. Yes. *'Follow me,'* " John whispered, in remembrance of the first call.

"Yes. *'Follow me.'* " Peter's voice was clear and steady. "Which one of us could ever forget the power of his *follow me*." He turned away from them and began walking.

"But wait!" Aaron shouted.

"Yes, wait for us!"

"I can't," said Peter. "I can no longer wait without the belief in his presence."

And John followed him as he'd never followed him before. And they followed him to seek the one who had been made flesh, once again, as it had been promised them in order for them to follow—or so they thought or heard or saw in their visions and their hope for the future of man, and woman, and . . .

HAMPTON ROADS PUBLISHING COMPANY

. . . for the evolving human spirit

Hampton Roads Publishing Company
publishes books on a variety of subjects including
metaphysics, health, visionary fiction,
and other related topics.

For a copy of our latest catalog,
call toll-free, 800-766-8009,
or send your name and address to:

Hampton Roads Publishing Company, Inc.
1125 Stoney Ridge Road
Charlottesville, VA 22902
e-mail: hrpc@hrpub.com
www.hrpub.com